Conten

Chapter 1
Dad on Breakfast-time TV and Dennis's Mad Dash

You know when something exciting happens first thing in the morning and you just can't wait to get to school and tell your friends?

But then your rabbit, Dennis, kicks orange juice all over your big sister's school bag and she gets in a bad mood and says, 'What friends?'

Well, that's what happened to me the day that Dad got on breakfast-time TV.

It was still dark outside when I woke up but there was a strip of light under the door so I knew someone else was already up. It couldn't be Primrose because she's as sluggish as a sloth first thing in the morning. I read about sloths in Animals of the World. They move so slowly they actually get moss growing on them – true story.

I put my dressing-gown and slippers on and went downstairs. There was no-one in the sitting room, which is on the floor below my and Primrose's bedrooms, so I went on down the next flight of stairs to the kitchen. All the houses in Harbour Row are very tall and thin.

Mum was sitting at the table eating a slice of toast.

'You're up nice and early,' she said. 'Well, I suppose it isn't every day a person's dad gets on breakfast-time TV!'

She got up to put some more toast on. 'I just hope he makes it. You know what he's like.'

One of Dad's favourite mottos is 'Better late than having to set the alarm,' so the chance of him getting to the studios by seven wasn't high. I was actually half hoping he wouldn't manage it because, under the circumstances, he would almost certainly make a fool of himself if he did.

'I'd better wake Primrose up,' Mum said, glancing at the clock. 'She'd hate to miss it.'

She went off upstairs and I gave Dennis a corner of my toast. Rabbits are supposed to like lettuce and leaves but he prefers bread and biscuits. Maybe it's an indoor-rabbit thing.

When Mum came back down she made some tea and we took it upstairs to the sitting room to drink in front of the TV. We shut the stair gate so Dennis couldn't come up. He mostly lives in the kitchen because it's one hundred per cent rabbit-proof, unlike the rest of the house. Dad's made gates across the front and back doors as well as the stairs, to keep him in.

The book says rabbits are fully house-trainable, which is true. What the book doesn't tell you is that your fully-house-trained rabbit is like a chewing-machine. He'll nibble through anything he can get to – furniture, wires, floor-coverings, door frames. He'll even nibble the plaster off the corners of your walls.

It's like those giant ants on David Attenborough that march into your house and munch their way through until there's nothing left but a few sticks and a pile of rubble. I'm not saying Dennis has got that far yet, but he's definitely working on it.

'Primrose!' Mum yelled up to her again as there still wasn't any sound of movement from her bedroom. 'It's going to be on any minute!'

There was a crash and a loud groan, followed

by a grumble. A slow th...ump-th...ump on the stairs, and about fifty hours later, Primrose appeared. Her eyes were half-closed and her hair was all over the place.

'W-what's going on?'

'Dad's on breakfast-time TV – remember?' said Mum.

'Oh, yeah,' goes Primrose. 'Have I got time to get some breakfast?'

'If you're quick.'

Primrose quick? Fat chance! She staggered down to the kitchen, mumbling and rubbing her eyes. We heard her fumbling around. The programme started with some clips of what was coming up. Dad hadn't only got there in time – he was going to be the first one on the sofa.

Mum called down to Primrose that she'd better hurry up or she would miss it.

'Our first guest this morning is Dave Pinker, the man behind the "Dear Daphne" page on the Three Towns Gazette. Dave was last night voted Best Agony Aunt of the Year at the prestigious Association of Agony Aunts Annual Presentation Dinner!'

Primrose arrived just in time as the camera panned across to Dad. She had a bowl of cereal in one hand and a glass of orange juice in the other. She put the orange juice on the floor by her feet so she could eat the cereal – once she had geared herself up to it. Like I said, in the mornings Primrose is slo-o-o-o-w.

'So, Dave,' said the presenter. 'Congratulations on winning this award. What, would you say, is the secret of being a great agony aunt?'

'I don't really know,' Dad said, with a modest shrug.

It was true – he didn't have a clue. When Ed first told him he had to do the 'Dear Daphne' page because the real Daphne had gone missing he was all at sea. 'I'm a sports reporter,' he complained. 'I don't do touchy-feely.'

It was a spot of luck for him that Mr Kaminski next door took pity on him and offered to help out. Mr K ended up writing all the answers himself, so that all Dad had to do was check his spellings and stuff because his English isn't very good. Now that Gran had come back to Polgotherick, Dad didn't even have to do that.

'So would you say it's just something that comes naturally to some people?' asked the presenter. Dad nodded and smiled.

So far, so good, but then...

'Dave has kindly agreed to take your calls and emails live on air,' said the presenter as the number to call appeared across the bottom of the screen.

'That's not good,' Primrose said, picking up her spoon.

'Hmm,' agreed Mum.

The presenter said, 'While we're waiting for your calls to come in, let's go to some of Dave's fellow agony aunts who we spoke to at last night's dinner.'

They showed some clips of Dad getting his award and the interviewer moving among the tables against a background of flash photography and applause. 'Is Dave a worthy winner, would you say?'

'Ooh yes, dear,' said a wrinkly lady in a twinkly tiara who was the agony aunt on the Yorkshire Chronicle.

'It's lovely to see a young person win for a change,' agreed a woman with pink lips and purple hair.

'And a man!' a third one chipped in. 'He's a real breath of fresh air.'

They all agreed that Dad had a surprising sense of humour. 'He gives such wise and serious advice to his readers, yet when you meet him in the flesh he's always joking around!'

'Omigod,' groaned Primrose, finally getting her spoon all the way to her mouth.

'And we've got our first caller!' exclaimed the presenter.

Just at that moment, Dennis appeared, looking like he'd lost a lettuce leaf and found a Rich Tea biscuit. He wasn't usually allowed in the sitting room unless someone was watching him. Primrose must have left the stair gate open, but none of us were about to tear ourselves away from Dad's big moment to put him back in the kitchen.

Dennis sniffed everyone's toes before flopping down in front of the TV. He likes Neighbours best but he isn't that fussy.

'My name's Sandy and I'm from Stafford,' the caller said.

'And what's the problem you'd like to put to our award-winning agony aunt?' asked the presenter.

'My problem is...' She lowered her voice to a whisper. 'Well, it's my husband, see? He's just retired from work and he sits around the house all day long watching TV like a proper old couch potato.'

Dad sighed and nodded in a wise kind of way. 'Has he always been just a little bit boring?' he asked.

There was a shocked silence from Sandy. Primrose groaned again and took another mouthful of cereal.

Luckily, Dad seemed to realise he was out of his depth and decided to play for time.

'This really is a tricky problem,' he said to the presenter.

The presenter looked at Dad expectantly. Dad didn't say anything. He just nodded and looked back at the presenter.

'S-so,' said the presenter, 'I suppose the advice here would be something like... maybe Sandy and her husband should try to find a new hobby they could both enjoy together?'

'Absolutely!'

'Something such as... golf, maybe?'

'Golf would be excellent,' agreed Dad.

It was a classic example of 'He who hesitates might get out of doing things' – another of Dad's favourite mottos. He's got hundreds of them.

'We've got another caller,' said the presenter. 'This is Baz from Brixton. What's your problem, Baz?'

'I've been going out with this girl for two years and she keeps banging on about us getting married. I mean, I like her and all that, but getting married is pretty major, am I right?'

Just then, Dennis sat up. His ears swivelled like two antennae. He must have picked up a noise from outside the window. He leapt up in the air and shot round the room like a lunatic, first one way and then the other. Mad dashes round the room are another thing your fully house-trained rabbit is inclined to do.

Smack! He crashed into Primrose's glass.

Splash! The orange juice sprayed up and came back down all over her new white school bag (which she shouldn't leave lying around).

Primrose went ballistic. I yelled at her to be quiet. 'I can't hear Dad!'

'Mum's recording it,' goes Primrose. 'You can see it later. Look what Dennis has done to my school bag!'

I grabbed Dennis and took him downstairs to wash his feet – he looked like he was wearing orange slippers. Mum got some soapy water to clean up the mess on the carpet. Primrose just sat there mumbling and grumbling. Considering it was her fault for leaving the stair gate open and not moving her glass off the floor when Dennis came bouncing in, that was quite annoying, but when you've got a big sister like Primrose you get used to feeling quite annoyed.

By the time all the orange juice was cleared up, Dad's interview was over and it was some boy and his friend who had found a box of old coins under a tree. Mum put the DVD on Play.

By some miracle, Dad managed to get through another two calls without actually offering any answers at all, and the only time he tried to make a suggestion it was so wrong the interviewer thought he was joking. I mean, no-one but Dad would think a sensible solution for a caller who didn't like housework was to move when it got too bad.

I was so relieved I felt like skipping as Primrose and me set off up the zig-zag path on the way to school. But Primrose was definitely not in a skipping mood. She was still peeved and prickly because of her stained school bag. She said it looked like someone had peed on it.

'I can't wait to tell my friends about Dad being on TV!' I said.

'What friends?' said Prickly Primrose.

Chapter 2
A Pair of Misfits and Matching-set Friends

Have you noticed how bad moods can be catching, like colds? I shouldn't try to talk to Primrose when she's in a mood because she just puts me in one too, but I never remember.

'What do you mean, "What friends?" I've got lots of friends!'

'Like who?' goes Primrose.

It was chilly even for November. There was frost on the edges of the path and our breath puffed out like clouds in the air. The houses in Old Polgotherick were built before cars were invented so there aren't any roads, just steep zig-zag paths that wind up between the houses from the harbour to the main road at the top.

'Like Toby and Jess,' I said.

Primrose did a funny sort of snort.

'What's that supposed to mean?'

'It means those two are a pair of misfits,' she said. 'They aren't proper friends, are they?'

We stopped at the Old Bakery to catch our breath. The boats in the harbour were as still as a picture and the sea looked glassy and grey. The seagulls seemed super-noisy in the cold, still air, as if someone had turned the volume up.

I let the misfits part go, but I didn't see how she could say they weren't proper friends. Toby and Jess were the two people I always talked to if I had a problem or if something brilliant happened, like Dad being on TV and managing not to fall flat on his face.

'They can't be proper friends because you don't do proper-friends things with them,' she went on. 'You don't go round each other's houses after school or hang out at the beach or go round the shops, do you? You don't really even hang out together at school.'

It was true we hardly saw each other at school

but that was because we all went to different lunchtime clubs and stuff. It was also true that I had never been to Jess's house and generally tried not to go to Toby's.

Toby's dad was in charge of the Polgotherick Cubs and Scouts and his mum ran the Brownies and Guides; when you sat down to eat your tea with them you felt like you were going for your table manners badge.

So I didn't like going round his house, but in an outdoors situation Toby's family didn't feel so full-on, and that was handy considering they spent most of their time outdoors. They did exciting things like night-hiking and winter camping, and they often asked me along.

'We do hang out at weekends,' I said. 'I went badger-watching with Toby's family last Saturday night!'

'Not exactly normal friends stuff, is it?' goes Primrose. 'And it isn't as if you and Toby and Jess ever do things together. Not like a proper group.'

'Actually, we're doing the Young Voices competition,' I said smugly, as if we were always teaming up for that kind of thing. 'Toby's the Chair, Jess is doing the speech, and I'm giving the vote of thanks.'

'Whatever,' goes Primrose. 'You know I'm right.'

'No you're not, and anyway, I've got lots of other friends.'

She did that stupid snort-thing again and didn't bother to say anything, and that's when I noticed that I'd caught her bad mood.

I tried to shake it off when I got to school.

'Hi Jess – did you see my dad on breakfast TV?'

Jess marked her place with her finger and looked up from her book.

'We don't watch TV before school. Why was he on?'

I told her he had just been voted Agony Aunt of the Year. She looked suitably impressed... and astonished.

'Your dad's an agony aunt? Why didn't you tell us?'

'He didn't want anyone to know. It's not really good for his image, being a sports reporter and all that.'

'I wonder what proportion of agony aunts are men,' Jess pondered. 'I'll look it up.'

That's what Jess does – she finds out facts and hoovers them up like an ant-eater hoovering up ants.

'Is Toby here yet?' I asked, looking around.

Kirsty overheard me.

'He's away – he's probably got pneumonia in his knees!'

Everyone burst out laughing. They all laugh at Toby because he sometimes wears shorts to school, even in the winter. He doesn't care. He says he prefers shorts and it isn't against school rules, so why shouldn't he? But I can't help wishing he wouldn't.

Just then, Sasha arrived with Tammy and Abina. They're the cool girls in our class and they don't usually take much notice of me.

Sasha's the prettiest girl in school. She's got honey-coloured hair that she ties back with flowers and stuff. Tammy's mum and dad own half the holiday homes on Mill Lane and she wears something new every single week. Abina's family moved here from Africa before she was born and they take her there on holiday every year. She's seen real live elephants and lions in the wild – imagine!

'We saw your dad on TV,' Sasha said. 'We thought he was brilliant!' They always say 'we'. They're like matching-set friends.

'We didn't even know he was an agony aunt. That's so cool!' said Tammy.

'We want to hear all about it!' said Abina.

They were serious. They thought Dad was some kind of celebrity. 'We never knew he was famous,' they said. They wanted to hear all about the twinkly dinner and the swanky London hotel and I told them everything I knew – except the fact that Dad didn't actually write the 'Dear Daphne' page. That was one of those accidental secrets that sometimes seem to get stuck.

It started because Mr Kaminski didn't want anyone to know he was the one doing it. 'I haf no qualification,' he said. Mum kept telling him he had all the qualifications he needed from studying in the School of Life for about a hundred years.

In the meantime, Dad's editor was amazed how brilliant Dad had turned out to be at solving people's problems, and now it was just too late for him to tell the truth.

Abina said, 'Wasn't it great when your dad told that man to get a new house if his old one was full of clutter?' They could remember every detail of the interview.

'Hey!' Sasha said. 'Why don't you come round my house after school and we can watch it again?'

'We always go to Sasha's on Mondays,' said Tammy.

I felt the way Dad must have done when they announced he'd won Agony Aunt of the Year. Could they mean me?

'I expect you're busy,' Abina said, seeing me glance round to check they weren't talking to someone else. 'What do you normally do on Mondays?'

What I normally did on Mondays was the same as every other day after school – watch Neighbours, mess about on the computer, play with Dennis, lie around on my bed reading... when you came to think about it, my life wasn't exactly action-packed.

'I'm not doing anything today,' I said. 'But I'll have to phone my mum.'

When I told Mum I was going to Sasha's after school she said I'd better let Primrose know. Dad works in the office on Mondays because the paper goes to press on Tuesdays, and Mum was going to be late back. When Mum and Dad aren't around, Primrose is supposed to be in charge.

I sent Primrose a text.

Won't be home – going to my friend Sasha's after school with other friends Tammy and Abina

So she thought I didn't have any proper friends? Well, that showed her!

Chapter 3
Sasha's after School and the Cat that got the Cream

Sasha's house was called 'Mariners' and it was right on the harbour. Inside, it was just like her mum's shop on Fore Street, full of old furniture painted in new colours, lacy cushions, candles and ornaments. It had big pictures on the walls and thick rugs on the floor.

We left our shoes at the door and went straight through to the kitchen. Everything was spotless.

Gran would have said you could eat your dinner off that floor. You would not want to eat anything off our kitchen floor, especially since we've had Dennis.

The boats were bobbing in the harbour right outside the windows. There were freshly-baked shortbread biscuits on a cooling-rack on the counter. Sasha told us to help ourselves while she poured some juice.

'Your mum's a great cook,' I said, trying not to sound jealous.

Sasha laughed. 'My mum doesn't cook! That's Margaret's job. She comes every day after school and stays till Mum gets home.'

Just then, Margaret put her head round the door to say hello. She had frizzy grey hair and a hearty look. She said if we didn't need anything she would carry on with the dusting.

There were two glass doors from the kitchen onto a balcony that jutted out over the water. Some of the other houses in the row had boats tethered to their balcony-rails and metal ladders going down to them. If Toby's family lived in Sasha's house they'd have a whole bunch of boats tied up outside and the balcony would be crammed with canoes.

I gave up trying not to sound jealous. 'You've got a great house.'

'It's all right,' said Sasha. 'But I wish we had a garden. You've got big gardens in Harbour Row. You're so lucky!'

I didn't tell her that in fact most of ours had been sold off to the house next door before we moved there, so all we actually had was a dark yard that hardly got any sunshine.

'Let's go and watch Peony's dad on TV again,' said Tammy.

Sasha's bedroom was three times bigger than mine and she had her own widescreen TV. I was a bit nervous in case I had missed any terrible gaffes the first time round, but on the second time of watching, Dad still did surprisingly well.

'You're so lucky having a dad like that,' they said. 'You must be able to talk to him about absolutely everything.'

I could hardly stop myself doing one of Primrose's famous snorts. Dad was great in lots of ways but if you wanted help with a problem you'd get more sense out of Dennis.

When we had watched Dad's interview they decided to put on a DVD. Sasha had the complete first series of Vampire Girl. I'd never seen any of it before so they started with Episode One.

'Everyone watches Vampire Girl,' they said. 'How come you've missed it?'

Vampires had always seemed a bit silly to me but I didn't like to say so, so I blamed it on Primrose. She has her uses!

'We've only got one TV,' I said, 'and my big sister hogs it.'

'You're so lucky having a big sister,' said Sasha.

'Yes,' agreed Abina. 'I've only got a little one.'

'And I've only got brothers,' said Tammy. 'All they talk about is football.'

They seemed to think a big sister was like a best friend, only better. I smiled and nodded. There wasn't any point in putting them straight. It wasn't as if they'd ever invite me again.

'What do you do on Wednesdays after school?' Sasha asked. 'We go to Tammy's. You can come too if you like.'

Abina told me their timetable. 'Sasha can't do Tuesdays because of dancing, Tammy can't do Thursdays because of orchestra and I can't do Fridays because of basketball, so we can only hang out on Mondays and Wednesdays after school. Then on Saturday afternoons we meet at mine.'

It was exactly like Primrose had said, friends going round each other's houses all the time – if this was really how the rest of the world did things, no wonder she thought I didn't have any proper friends.

We went home at about six o'clock. I walked some of the way with Tammy and Abina. It was nearly dark and the lights were twinkling on the water in the harbour. They put their arms round my waist as we walked, which felt kind of weird but nice. It wasn't the sort of thing Toby and Jess would do.

I split off from Tammy and Abina and went up the zig-zag path, getting to my house just in time to see Matt coming out. He is officially the best boyfriend Primrose has ever had, plus he's got the most adorable dog called Sam. He always brings Sam with him when he comes round our house, which is nearly every day, because he knows I love walking him.

Matt was standing at the bottom of our steps, waiting. Sam's very old so he only has two speeds – slow on the flat and super-slow on stairs.

'Are you going already?' I asked. 'I wanted to take Sam for a walk.'

I had lots to talk about and Sam was the best listener. He finally made it to the bottom of the steps and held his head up for me to stroke.

'Sorry,' said Matt. 'I've got to go. But your dad's just got home, so I don't suppose you'd want to go straight out again anyway.'

Mum, Dad and Primrose were in the kitchen, drinking fizzy apple juice out of champagne glasses. Mum poured some for me. Dennis had jumped up onto a chair and had his front paws on the table, which he isn't supposed to do. He was eating Dad's newspaper but no-one else seemed to have noticed.

'Hello Peony!' goes Dad, giving me a hug. 'What do you think about your old dad being Agony Aunt of the Year, then?'

He looked like the cat that got the cream. Or rather, the cat that ate all the sweets and made himself over-excited.

'I'm on the front page of the London Evening News – look!'

We all looked. Mum scooped Dennis up off the chair and put him down on the floor. She shook out what was left of the newspaper. Bits flew all over the place. Most of the front page was shredded.

'He's eaten it!' wailed Dad.

'I know what,' said Mum. 'Let's go upstairs and watch the DVD again!'

So I got to see Dad's interview for the third time, only this time he gave us a running commentary.

'That's Kay!' he said, pointing to the agony aunt with the pink lips and purple hair. 'She lives just up the road in Devon... Can you tell I'm wearing make-up...? See what I did there, I waited and he answered for me!'

'We saw that,' said Primrose. She was in a good mood again now, so she was enjoying Dad's interview much more than first time around. To be fair, since she's been going out with Matt she's nearly always in a good mood, except when she's just got out of bed. Then she's like a lion with toothache and you just have to keep out of her way.

When the interview finished, Dad said, 'I was good, wasn't I? I can't believe I nearly didn't go!'

There were two reasons why Dad hadn't wanted to go to the presentation dinner – one, he doesn't like doing anything that he doesn't have to do, and two, he didn't want his friends to find out that he'd been filling in for Daphne. It was embarrassing, he said, a sports reporter having to stand in for an agony aunt.

But Ed wouldn't let him get out of it. 'It'll be good publicity for the Three Towns Gazette and a free feed for you,' he'd said. 'That's what I call a win-win situation!'

Mum had told Dad not to worry. Although the dinner was going to be on TV there would be tons of people there – no-one would even notice him.

It had never crossed anyone's mind that he might actually win.

'Everyone will have seen me getting the award!' Dad said happily. It seemed that being an agony aunt was only embarrassing if you were average at it – if you were the best in the country, it suddenly wasn't embarrassing at all.

'It should really have been Mr Kaminski who won it,' said Mum.

'And Gran,' I said. 'She's been checking his spellings and stuff.'

Dad didn't seem to hear. He was busy switching on his laptop to see if he could find a copy of the picture Dennis had shredded on the London Evening News website.

Mum gave up and changed the subject. 'So you've got some new friends, Peony. Did you have a nice time at Sasha's?'

'I've got some new friends too,' Dad said, before I had a chance to answer. 'The other agony aunts – they love me! We're going to do video conferencing.'

'They only love you because they think you're Daphne,' Mum pointed out. 'And they'd only be "the other" agony aunts if you really were an agony aunt yourself.'

'Here I am!' cried Dad, finding the picture. He turned his laptop round so we could see it.

It looked as if being famous might be going to his head.

Chapter 4
Parsnip Pudding and
Perfect Happiness
(which are two different things)

Toby was still off school the next day and Jess had cello at lunchtime. Tammy and Abina were going to netball practice and Sasha asked me if I wanted to go along with her and watch. That's what they do. Even if they aren't all taking part, they go along and support each other.

It would never have crossed my mind to go and listen to Jess learning to play her cello, which just went to show how much I had to learn about having proper friends.

When I got home from school, Matt and Sam were already there and Primrose was making banana milkshakes. She put an extra banana in the food-mixer for me and sloshed in a bit more milk.

Whenever Matt was around, Primrose turned into the Best Big Sister in the World to impress him. It was just a shame that, knowing Primrose, it couldn't last. Sooner or later, she was bound to mess it up.

I took Sam for a walk down into town. It was a chilly day and he seemed to go even slower than usual. By the time we got to the harbour I was so cold I couldn't feel my face.

Walking back up the hill, I gave in and carried him most of the way. I put him down at the bottom of our steps and waited for him to start climbing up. But he looked at me in that steady way dogs look at you when they want something, and he didn't stop looking until I picked him up again.

I carried Sam up the steps. The lights were on in the house and the kitchen windows were all steamed up, so Mum must be home from work, cooking tea.

The upside of Mum having a gardening business was that she got home early every day in the winter. The downside was that she was too good at it – the gardens she looked after produced so much fruit and veg that people had started giving her boxes to bring home.

We had been working our way all week through a big box of parsnips someone had given her. In case you're lucky enough not to know, a parsnip looks like a carrot that's lost its colour and crunch. It's kind of greyish-cream and mostly turns to mush when you cook it, which wouldn't matter if it tasted nice.

Mum had made mushy parsnip chips, mushy parsnip crisps and mushy parsnip pie over the weekend, and we still had plenty of parsnips left for a few more days of pain.

I put Sam down on the rug in front of the radiator and he sat there looking sorry for himself. Dennis bounced over to give him a good sniff, but Sam ignored him.

'Poor thing,' said Mum. 'He doesn't like this cold weather.'

My face was beginning to thaw out.

'What are you making?' I asked.

'Parsnip pudding,' said Mum. Oh, joy!

I sat down on the rug next to Sam and scooped Dennis up onto my lap for his daily grooming

34

session. He used to wriggle when I tried to brush him but then I discovered all you have to do is hold your free hand close to his face, flat and low, and then he'll push his nose underneath it and keep completely still.

It says in You and Your Rabbit that if your rabbit leaps around rubbing things with his chin he's saying 'This is mine!', but if he puts his chin on the ground and dips his nose underneath your hand or the arch of your foot that means 'You're the boss,' and he stops leaping around and relaxes.

I was planning to put Dennis in the Polgotherick Pet Parade and that's why I was brushing him every day. I had three weeks to get him looking his absolute best. Not that he needed much help – he was naturally adorable!

For the last three years, Mrs Bolitho's parrot had won first prize in the pet parade, just because he could say 'Who's a pretty boy?' but he wasn't really that pretty any more. His feathers were looking tatty and he'd taken to sticking out his tongue, which was all black and leathery. There was no way the judges could choose him again, not with Dennis in the competition.

Dennis stayed calm even when Dad burst in, dumped his coat on the table with a flourish, and announced that he had had a brilliant day at work. Ed was delighted with him and everyone in the office thought he was the bee's knees.

'My mates from football have been texting me all day,' he said. 'They've been calling me Daphne!'

He was so excited he could hardly keep still.

'What's for supper, Jan? Parsnip pudding? My favourite!'

He was practically jumping up and down. It was just a shame the nose-under-hand thing didn't work with human beings.

There was a knock at the door and Gran walked in.

'Mum!' goes Dad, giving her a big hug. 'Did you see me on TV?'

Mum said, 'Are you staying for supper, Gwen? There's plenty to go round.'

Before Gran could answer, Mr Kaminski put his head round the door. He always seemed to arrive like magic whenever Gran came round. He was wearing a new green cardigan with a blue stripe down one sleeve, Dad's latest thank-you present for doing the problem page.

'Would you like to join us for supper, Mr Kaminski?' said Mum.

When it comes to eating parsnip pudding, you can do with all the help you can get, so it was good we had Matt, Gran and Mr Kaminski crammed in round the kitchen table with us when Mum got it out of the oven.

The parsnip pudding was puffed up like a pile of cotton wool, but as soon as Mum put it down on the mat it collapsed and went wrinkly.

'I see you on television, Dave,' said Mr Kaminski, as Mum started dishing up. 'You are very good. You are star!'

'I couldn't have done it without your help,' goes Dad.

What did he mean, without Mr Kaminski's help? He couldn't have done it without Mr Kaminski doing it!

We had mashed potatoes and cabbage with the parsnip pudding, which made three heaps of greyish mush. At times like this you've got to be grateful to the person who invented ketchup.

Dad talked about his TV adventure all the way through the meal and then Mum collected up the plates. She didn't seem to notice I had hidden most of my parsnip pudding under my knife and fork.

'I've got some exciting news myself,' Gran said, finally managing to get a word in edgeways. 'I'm getting the keys to my new house this weekend!'

'The sale has gone through?' cried Mum. 'That's fantastic!'

Everyone gave Gran a hug, even Matt and

Mr Kaminski. Actually, Mr Kaminski gave her an especially big hug.

'Is wonderful,' he said, finally letting her go. 'We do boat trips now, yes?'

That was the plan. Gran had given up teaching old people to surf in St Ives and was coming back to live in Polgotherick. She was going to run boat trips round the harbour, and Mr Kaminski was going to help. Gran had lots of great plans but they didn't all work out, so I hoped Mr Kaminski wasn't going to be disappointed.

'I can't wait to get my hands on that garden!' said Mum.

Gran's new house was only a few minutes' walk from ours, over the stile at the top of Harbour Row and out on the coastal path. It had been empty for ages and the garden was like a jungle. It was called Nash House.

'I won't be able to move in until the workmen have done the central heating and everything,' Gran said. 'But Jane says I can stay as long as I like at the Happy Haddock.'

Jane was Gran's old school friend and she ran the pub at the far end of the harbour. I thought, 'I bet Jane was the kind of friend who went along to watch when Gran had swimming club and stuff.' I wondered if me and Sasha would still be friends when we were a squillion years old.

After everyone had gone I sat on the floor in front of the radiator again and Dennis came lolloping over. I held my hand close to the ground. He pushed his nose underneath my fingers and I gently stroked his side with my other hand.

Everything was perfect. Dad was famous, Mum's business was going well, Primrose was in a good mood. Gran was moving back to Polgotherick and Dennis was going to win the top prize at the pet parade. As well as Toby and Jess, now the coolest girls in the class wanted to be friends with me.

Life was good, like a big shiny bubble. But the problem with bubbles is, they burst.

Chapter 5
Heavenly Honeybun and the Winning Team

The Young Voices competition was only a few weeks away and we hadn't had a single practice. Jess got into a stress because Toby was still off school and we didn't know when he'd be back. It turned out he'd fallen off a wall at the weekend and hurt his ankle.

'How long does a sprained ankle take to get better?' she said. 'And why does he have to keep doing such stupid things?'

That seemed a bit harsh considering it wasn't a very big wall. He just landed badly.

I said, 'Don't worry, he'll be fine, he's really good at public speaking.'

This was true. Last year we had got through to the regional semis with Toby's talk on Sir Hugh Munro, who made a list of all the highest mountains in Scotland and then tried to climb them. He would have managed it too, if he hadn't died just before the one he was saving for last. That's got to be the definition of bad luck.

We bagged the bench at the far side of the tennis courts at lunchtime and Jess read me her speech. It was called 'Five Fascinating Facts.' Jess likes facts and she likes fives. She lives in a house called Five Trees and collects sets of five facts in her notebook.

'Five is the perfect number of facts,' said Jess, reading from her notes. 'It's not too many so you get confused, but it's enough to make you feel you know something worth knowing...'

Her speech included five fascinating facts about the Young Voices competition. It was really clever and interesting, and that's what I was planning to say in my vote of thanks.

We ran through it again to make double-sure it was the right length and then we walked back across the playground together. I told her about going to Sasha's house on Monday and how Sasha, Tammy and Abina had regular days for going round each other's houses.

'Tonight they're going to Tammy's. Actually, I'm going too. You don't mind, do you?'

I didn't want Jess to think I wasn't still friends with her, just because I was hanging out with other people too.

'Why should I mind?' she said.

I told her about going along to watch the netball and doing things just to support each other in that matching-set kind of way.

'It sounds a bit boring, just watching,' she said. 'I know five facts about netball – would you like to hear them?'

It turned out Jess also knew five facts about Polgotherick Mill when I told her that was where Tammy lived. It wasn't a mill any more, but the big wheel was still there on the side of the house, and so was the stream. You had to go over a little footbridge to get to the front door. I couldn't wait for school-out.

Tammy's dad picked us up in his seven-seater and we all piled into the back.

I don't know how, but we got talking about

Dennis. They thought it was odd, him living indoors.

'What about all his pees and poos?' said Tammy.

'He does them in his litter tray,' I said. 'Rabbits are fully house-trainable.'

'But if they were supposed to be indoors they wouldn't have all that fur,' Sasha said.

'It can't be healthy for him,' agreed Abina.

'He's very healthy,' I said, sticking up for him. 'He's in tip-top condition! I'm putting him in the Polgotherick Pet Parade and I think he's going to win.'

'You'll have to show Peony your rabbit, Tammy,' her dad said, over his shoulder.

Tammy's rabbit lived in a shed at the bottom of her garden. She was called Heavenly Honeybun. As soon as we got to Tammy's house, we went to see her.

Heavenly Honeybun didn't look anything like Dennis. She didn't look like a normal rabbit at all.

'She's a Blue French Angora,' Tammy said proudly, not taking her out of her hutch.

Heavenly Honeybun had short, dark-grey fur on her face, but from the neck down her fur was long, fluffy and white. She looked like a grey rabbit wearing a sheepskin jacket.

I wanted to pick her up but Tammy said she

didn't like being handled. They had to wear heavy-duty gardening gloves to groom her.

'You know what would be fun?' Tammy said, as we picked some grass to push through the mesh. 'I could put Heavenly Honeybun in the pet parade too!'

'I think it might be too late to enter now,' I said, really hoping it was.

We had a snack and then did a fitness DVD. Tammy said they always did fitness and homework at her house on Wednesdays, just the same as they always watched Vampire Girl on Mondays at Sasha's.

Having a schedule for homework was a much better system than mine. I always did my homework at the last minute and if something nice came up such as, for example, Gran coming over, I accidentally-on-purpose forgot it. No wonder Sasha, Tammy and Abina always came top in tests.

When we had finished our homework, they decided to practise their Young Voices presentation.

'You can watch,' Sasha said. 'You can tell us what you think.'

Abina introduced her, and then Sasha did her talk. She must have practised loads of times because she didn't even have any notes.

'The subject of my talk is The World of Fashion...'

After she had finished, Abina invited questions from the audience, which was me. I managed to think of a few, and Sasha answered them perfectly. Then Tammy did the vote of thanks, and that was perfect too. It was all perfect.

They were obviously going to win. They won at everything. They were always the winning team. And that was fair, because they worked so hard to win. Not like me and Jess and Toby.

'You're doing the vote of thanks for Jess, aren't you?' Sasha said. 'She's very nice, isn't she... but just a little bit strange?'

They hadn't even heard her talk yet!

'And is Toby your Chair?' asked Abina. 'Why does he wear those shorts?'

They weren't being nasty, just saying facts, the way David Attenborough might say, 'This eyeless mud-sucking fish is the ugliest creature on the planet' and not sound mean.

By the time I got home I was feeling a bit flat. So was Dad. The novelty was beginning to wear off and he was getting fed up with everyone calling him Daphne.

'They'll stop soon,' Mum told him, flicking through her parsnip recipes.

'Is Matt still here?' I said. I wanted to take Sam

for a walk and think about things.

'Yes, he's upstairs watching TV with Primrose.'

'So... where's Sam?'

Whenever Matt was at our house Sam stayed in the kitchen because he didn't like climbing the stairs.

'Matt's decided not to bring him round any more for the time being,' Mum said. 'How about parsnip fritters?'

My eyes suddenly felt prickly.

'What do you mean, Matt's not bringing him round any more?'

'His joints stiffen up in the cold weather so Matt thinks he'd be better staying home by the fire,' she said. 'You can still see him every week at the kennels.'

Matt's family, the Teversons, owned the kennels in Hayden's Lane and I worked there, cleaning out the pens and walking the dogs on Saturday mornings.

'Why don't you do Dennis's grooming?' said Mum.

I got Dennis's brush and sat down on the floor by the radiator. He came lolloping over to sniff me. I scooped him up onto my lap. He was cute and cuddly but he wasn't a wise old friend like Sam. He was soft and adorable but he wasn't a fancy rabbit like Heavenly Honeybun. I couldn't help feeling just the teeniest weeniest bit disappointed in Dennis.

A bit later though, Dennis was everyone's hero. Well, everyone's except Mum's. She had put the box of parsnips on the floor beside the sink while she was looking through her recipes.

'So parsnip fritters it is then,' she said, 'with a nice brown onion sauce.'

She picked up the box and the bottom fell out. Wet parsnips crashed onto the floor.

'Dennis has peed in the parsnips!' she cried.

So we never did get parsnip fritters. We had to have pizza instead.

Chapter 6
Becky's Tombola and Pookie the Pig

I told Sam about Dennis peeing in the parsnips. I was lying beside him on the floor in front of the stove in the Teversons' kitchen, stroking his wiry fur. Becky, the other Saturday helper, had said I could go in and see him while she was finishing up.

There was no-one else around. Matt was at our house, his brothers were making hay-bale tunnels in the barn, and Mrs Teverson was outside talking to some people about their dog.

'I don't know what Sasha, Tammy and Abina would say if they knew Dennis peed in the parsnips,' I said to Sam. 'I told them he was fully house-trained!'

Sam's tail thumped on the floor. Matt was probably right – he did seem happier staying home in the warm.

'They already think Dennis should live out of doors,' I said. 'Sasha says if rabbits were meant to live in the house they wouldn't have all that thick fur.'

I stroked Sam's sides, and his silky-smooth ears. They're the only part of him that hasn't gone wiry and grey. I caught his eye and it felt like he was saying to me, 'Hold on a minute – that's mad! Dogs and cats are covered in fur too, but no-one thinks they should sleep outside!'

That's the great thing about talking to Sam – you can kind of see what he's thinking. I gave him a big hug, burying my face in his neck. It was going to be hard only seeing him once a week, but it would have been a lot harder if I couldn't see him at all.

Becky opened the door, kicked off her boots and came in. She had finished cleaning out the last pen and walking the last dog. Her short spiky hair was sticking out on one side from where she had pulled off her hat.

'Ready when you are,' she told me, bending down to give Sam a pat.

In the summer we used to go to the beach cafe for a pasty when we finished at the kennels but the cafe was closed up for the winter so we'd started going to Becky's for a sandwich instead. Her house was on my way home.

Becky was older than me but she was living proof that not all teenagers were moody like Primrose – Mum really should stop saying it was just her hormones whenever she went off on one.

Becky was also proof that teenagers weren't just interested in boys and shopping, like you-know-who. She wanted to work for the RSPCA when she grew up, saving abandoned animals and stuff. She was having a tombola stall at the Polgotherick Pet Parade to raise money for them.

'It's the perfect opportunity,' she said. 'Everyone who goes to a pet parade is bound to be an animal-lover – my stall will make a fortune!'

I was helping her to get the prizes. I already had a copy of next year's Three Towns Gazette calendar from Dad, a mini Christmas tree in a pot from Mum and a recipe book from Gran – she had bought it and then remembered she already had a copy at home.

Me and Becky walked down the lane and over

the stile into the fields behind her house. It was a bright day but there was still frost under the hedges where the sun didn't reach.

'Is Dennis ready for the big day?' she said.

'Yes... I guess.'

'What's wrong?'

I told her about Tammy's fancy Blue French Angora.

'If Tammy puts Heavenly Honeybun in the pet parade, Dennis hasn't got a hope,' I said.

'Looks aren't everything,' said Becky.

There was a parcel from the RSPCA waiting for her when we got back to her house. It was full of free leaflets and car stickers, pens, bookmarks and badges to put on her stall.

'I was thinking of making some posters,' she said, 'and a big sign-board to stand beside the table.'

She asked if I would like to stay and help her after lunch. Normally, I'd have loved to. But Sasha, Tammy and Abina were meeting at Abina's house at two-thirty, and they had invited me. I hardly had time to finish my sandwich before I had to go.

Becky didn't mind.

'We could do it next week,' she suggested. 'I could come down to yours afterwards and do a practice pet parade with Dennis. I'll be the judges and ask you lots of questions.'

This sounded like such a good idea, it almost seemed a shame I'd probably be at Abina's again.

Abina lived in one of the big new houses on the top road. It was only a five-minute walk from Becky's, and I got there just before Sasha. On the driveway, Abina and Tammy were passing a netball to each other and shooting at a hoop above the garage door.

'Have you showed Peony Pookie yet?' asked Sasha. 'She's going to love him!'

They all grinned at each other.

'Come on!' they said together, in their matching-set way.

The back garden was a big square, divided in half by a wire fence. On our side of the fence there was a lawn with a few small trees; on the other side was bare earth... and a pot-bellied pig!

He grunted excitedly when he saw us and galloped up to the gate. He was about the same size as a Labrador or Golden Retriever, only much fatter. His skin was pink except for black patches across his face and shoulders and back legs, and thinly covered with bristles.

'Sit, Pookie,' Abina said, and he sat down.

'Stay,' she said, as she opened the gate.

Abina stroked and patted Pookie as if he was a dog, and then Sasha and Tammy joined in.

'He won't bite!' Abina said to me, over her shoulder.

I patted his head and he fixed me with his little round eyes.

'Pigs are the fourth cleverest animals in the world,' Abina said, proudly. 'After humans, monkeys and dogs. Show us your house,' she said to Pookie, and he trotted off down the garden with all of us following.

Pookie's house was a stone shed with a nest of wood shavings in one corner. Abina unhooked a dog's lead from the back of the door and put it on him. We walked him up to the gate, across the lawn and round the front to the drive. He was as good as gold. He didn't pull or anything.

Abina gave the lead to Tammy and told us to give her five minutes. We walked Pookie up and down the drive until she came back.

'I've hidden some f-o-o-d scraps in Pookie's patch,' she said, spelling it out, as if he would understand if she said the word.

'What kind of food does he eat?' I asked, not thinking.

As soon as I said the word 'food', he was off. Tammy couldn't control him. She had to let go of the lead. Pookie raced down the garden, shot through the gate and rooted around in the earth with his snout, sniffing and grunting like mad.

'Pot-bellied pigs do like their food,' Abina said, laughing. 'They can sniff out a sweet at a hundred metres.'

Pookie found all his titbits in about three minutes flat. He had a last sniff around, and then trotted back to us. He sat down in front of Abina and lifted his face for her to stroke him under the chin.

I wanted to stay and play with Pookie but Sasha, Tammy and Abina always did an hour of netball practice on Saturdays. Tammy and Abina both played defence on the school team so me and Sasha had to be shooters, and I can't shoot for toffee.

'Keep trying,' they said, to encourage me. 'If at first you don't succeed, try, try, try again.'

I told them Dad's version was, 'If at first you don't succeed, give up!'

'He sounds funny!' they said. 'We can't wait to meet him.'

When I told them he was serious, they didn't believe me. They said I was funny too. Then Sasha asked me what I did on Sundays. That was the only day they were all free, she said.

I suddenly realised that if I was going to be friends with Sasha, Tammy and Abina they would expect to come to my house too. I would have to have my own regular day.

I imagined what they would think when they saw our chewed-up kitchen, with Dennis doing his mad dashes and digging in his litter-tray. Or when I took them upstairs to the sitting room and they met Primrose, all lovey-dovey with Matt on the settee or stropping around on her own.

I pictured their faces when they saw my bedroom with its wall of dogs (I had sixty breeds now, all the best pictures I could find, with the name and description underneath). Sasha had models on her bedroom wall; Abina had sports stars; and Tammy had a few family photos in frames.

What would they think when they got their first whiff of Mum's cooking? No-one else in the world would ever make cabbage curry or turnip tart. And then there was Dad. As soon as they met him they would know he was no agony aunt – he was a total fraud!

One thing was for sure. I could not let my new friends see my house or meet my family. I was going to have to think up a seriously good excuse.

Chapter 7
Dennis the Menace and Too Much Teasing

Dennis only goes in his hutch to eat and sleep but on Sunday mornings, when I try to clean it out, he gets all territorial. He thumps his back feet on the floor and growls. He bares his teeth and runs at me. He's a real menace.

His hutch is in the gap under the stairs and the first few times I tried to clean it out I kept bumping my head trying to get away from him. I had to develop a technique.

Now I put my hand near the ground till he comes and pushes his nose under it, then I switch over and put my foot where my hand was, and keep it there while I clear the old newspaper and hay into a bin bag and empty his food bowl for washing.

As soon as I move my foot, Dennis leaps on the bin bag and digs around in it like he's lost something. I guess that if a huge giant were to come along and empty everything out of our house into a massive bin bag, I might do the same.

I wash his food and water bowls, put new newspaper on the floor of his hutch and fetch some fresh hay. Then I fill his water bowl again and pour some new rabbit mix into his food bowl.

As soon as I've finished, he forgets about the bin bag and jumps up into his hutch. He kicks the clean hay around in the bedroom end, then tips the food bowl over with his teeth, scattering rabbit mix all over the clean newspaper and across the kitchen floor.

'Why does he do that?' Primrose said, looking up from her breakfast. The rest of us had already had lunch but Primrose hibernates like a hedgehog at weekends.

I shrugged. Rabbits were not famous for their brain power. In the league table of world's cleverest animals they definitely wouldn't be up there with dogs and pigs.

'Dennis!' I said sharply, when he started trying to rip the clean newspaper out from underneath him. He stopped and stared at me. Then – boing! He bounced out of his hutch and shot round the room like a firework in a barrel.

I swept the new food up and put it back in his bowl.

Primrose said, 'Where's Mum?'

'Putting a trellis up in the Peace Garden. I don't know where Dad is, though.'

'I saw him in the living-room with his laptop,' Primrose said. 'He's setting up his conference call with the agony aunts.'

She dumped her cereal bowl in the sink and put the kettle on.

'Matt says his mum said to tell you that you don't have to rush off after work on Saturdays – you can stay as long as you like and talk to Sam.'

I explained that I hadn't had much time the day before because of going to Abina's.

'I felt bad leaving Sam so soon, and then I had to rush off straight after lunch from Becky's so I couldn't help her with her poster. I felt bad about that too.'

'I wouldn't worry about it,' Primrose said. 'It's not as if Becky's really a proper friend. She's just someone you work with, isn't she?'

'I go round her house every week,' I protested. 'That's what you said proper friends do.'

Primrose tipped some hot choc powder into her cup, poured hot water on it and stirred.

'You only go round there because it's on your way home. Ask yourself this – would Becky still ask you round if you didn't work at the kennels together?'

I asked myself, but before I could come up with an answer, Dad called us to go up and meet his new friends.

Primrose groaned. 'I'm not even dressed,' she muttered. 'What are they going to think?'

'Just cough a bit. They'll think you've got flu.'

That gave me an idea! If Sasha and the others wanted to come to my house next Sunday I could say Primrose had something catching.

Cough, cough! Primrose practised on the way upstairs. Dad said, 'Here come my lovely daughters.' He turned the laptop round so his friends could see us coming through the door. Three agony aunts smiled and waved at us from their separate windows on the screen.

'This is Primrose. She's fifteen,' Dad said, proudly.

Primrose coughed and pulled her dressing gown tighter. She gave a little wave and said hello, sounding suitably feeble.

'Have you got a cold, dear?' asked the first agony aunt.

I recognised her from the breakfast show. She was the one with the pink lips and purple hair who'd said it was lovely to see a young person win for a change. Young? Dad? He said she was called Kay.

'You should go back to bed and keep warm,' said the second agony aunt. She was what Gran would call plain as a pudding, with brown hair, a brown top and brown wooden beads. Dad said she was called Alice.

'I'm Jeannie,' said the third, wobbling her chins. 'You go and snuggle under the duvet, Primrose. I'm sure that lovely little sister of yours will bring you up some toast.'

It was Dad's cue to introduce me.

'This is Peony.'

'Hello, Peony,' the agony aunts said together.

It was cringe central for the next few seconds but we were saved by the front door bell. I went down to see who it was and Primrose scuttled gratefully off upstairs to get dressed.

Dennis was sitting in the middle of the kitchen floor, not hiding, so it must be someone he knew. His ears were cocked forward, listening. One of them swivelled round as I walked in, but he didn't turn his head.

I could hear them now, chatting on the doorstep. It was Gran and Jane.

'Look what I've got!' Gran said, as she walked in. She jangled a set of keys in the air. 'Who wants to come and have a look round my new house?'

While we were waiting for Dad to come off the computer and Primrose to get ready, Mr Kaminski arrived. He said he had just come to borrow some sugar.

'We're going to see my new house,' Gran told him. 'Come with us if you aren't too busy baking.'

As we walked up the zig-zag path, Gran asked Dad about his video conference. It evidently hadn't been what he was expecting. He had thought they were just going to chat about the dinner and tell him how brilliant he was again, but it turned out they had a conference call every Sunday to talk about work.

The agony aunts would read each other their letters and discuss the best way to answer them. This was obviously not ideal for Dad, as he never actually read the letters or wrote the answers, so when it was his turn he decided to distract them by coming up with a problem of his own. He told them about his workmates and pub friends teasing him about being an agony aunt and calling him Daphne.

'Is that a problem?' asked Gran.

Dad said, actually, as it turned out, it was. 'I never realised, but Kay says too much teasing can be bad for a person's self-esteem.'

'Is that how you feel about it – like your self-esteem has taken a knock?'

'I don't know,' said Dad. 'I can't really tell. Anyway, then Alice said, "These people are supposed to be your friends!" and Jeannie said my friends must have very poor people skills.'

Dad had never even heard of people skills before and he was pretty sure he'd never had any friends who had them until he met Kay, Alice and Jeannie. They were really nice. They were coming all the way to Polgotherick to take him out for lunch. That was how nice they were!

We went over the stile at the first bend and started along the coastal path. Up ahead, Nash House stood behind its high stone wall, looking out to sea like a shabby old sailor. Its white walls were dirty and peeling, and its porch was falling away.

Gran unlocked the padlock on the boarded-up gate to let us in. The garden was a complete wreck. Inside, the house was even worse. Wallpaper was hanging off the walls and the window frames were rotten.

'I won't be able to move in for a while,' Gran said.

'You can stay with me for as long as you like,' said Jane. 'There's always a room for you at the Happy Haddock, Gwennie!'

Mr Kaminski said we would soon get everything shipshape. When the builders had finished we could organise a working weekend. Mum and Stella could sort out the garden and the rest of us could do the decorating.

Dad said unfortunately he had to go to matches every weekend and write reports for the paper, but he was sure we would manage fine without him. I couldn't see Primrose being up for it, either.

Cough, cough! She had a little practice as we explored the rooms upstairs.

Chapter 8
Breathe in and Breathe out

Dad's got a sign on his study wall that says, 'Important things I have to do today – breathe in, breathe out.'

Sometimes Mum sticks post-its over it so it says stuff like, 'Important things I have to do today – sort out recycling, fix leaky tap, take wife out for dinner.'

When Primrose tries to get out of doing the dishes or clearing up her things, Mum says Dad's lazy attitudes must have rubbed off on her.

No-one usually says that about me, but as soon as I started hanging out with Sasha, Tammy and Abina, I could see it might be true.

What had I been doing with all my time? I never realised I was such a slacker until I started doing useful things 24:7 – keeping up with the cool shows on TV, handing in my homework, doing keep-fit DVDs, practising my netball skills and going to sports and activities in every single school break, even if I was only watching.

Being friends with Sasha, Tammy and Abina wasn't only fun – it was good for me. It was turning me into a better person.

I said that to Toby and Jess when we were looking for somewhere quiet to practise our Young Voices.

'I think you're fine just as you are,' Toby said.

His ankle was bandaged up and he had to walk with crutches, but he could go quite fast on them. People yelled 'Howdy, Hopalong!' and 'Nice shorts!' at him as he swung himself across the playground. He didn't take any notice.

We found an empty picnic table and sat down. Toby did his introduction and Jess did her talk. Every time I heard it, it sounded a little more weird. Why couldn't she have chosen a more normal subject, such as the World of Fashion, for example?

Toby thought her talk was awesome, but then he was a person who wore shorts to school in the middle of November. If he could get himself some friends like Sasha, Tammy and Abina, maybe that would be good for him too.

On Saturday I told Becky how being friends with Sasha, Tammy and Abina was making me a better person.

'They're good at everything,' I said. 'Even their pets are perfect!'

I told her about Pookie. I said how clever and well-trained he was, and how he didn't smell at all, like pigs are supposed to.

'I've never seen a pot-bellied pig,' Becky said. 'Maybe I could catch a glimpse of him today if you take him out for a walk. I've got to go up that way to put a poster in Rick's Garage.'

Rick's Garage was just past Abina's house on the main road so after lunch Becky decided to tag along with me. As we got near, we saw Sasha and Tammy coming towards us. I slowed down, hoping they would go straight in, but they waited for me at the end of her drive, and Abina came bounding out with her netball to greet them.

I suddenly saw Becky through their eyes. She was a foot taller than me, her short hair was sticking out all over the place and she was wearing a fake-fur coat she found in a charity shop – she always gets her clothes in charity shops because of saving the planet.

I remembered what Primrose said about Becky being too old to be my friend. I hoped they wouldn't think she was some kind of babysitter or something, like I wasn't allowed to walk up to Abina's on my own.

Sasha, Tammy and Abina said hello. I didn't introduce Becky. She hesitated a moment and then started on up towards the garage.

'Who's your friend?' said Sasha, as we turned into Abina's drive.

'She's not really my friend,' I said. 'We just work together at the kennels.'

I glanced over my shoulder and found Becky looking back at me. I knew, from the look on her face, that she had overheard what I said. She turned and walked away.

I didn't have time to worry about it because we straight away started our netball practice. They said they always did netball first and then went to see Pookie – they had only done it the other way round the week before because it was my first week and they knew I was nuts about animals.

'Your shooting's getting better,' Abina said, and they all agreed.

'It'll be so cool when you and Sasha get in the team,' said Tammy.

I had never been in the team for anything and I liked the sound of it. I didn't even mind when we did an extra twenty minutes, even though my legs were shaking from being so tired and my shots were falling further and further short of the hoop.

We went inside for a drink and a snack. We had to completely finish our biscuits before we went to see Pookie. As soon as he saw us he ran up to the fence, grunting loudly.

'Sit, Pookie,' Abina said as she unlatched the gate.

Pookie rolled over onto his back and let us stroke his fat tummy. He shut his little round eyes, lapping up the attention.

'Mum says I can put Heavenly Honeybun in the Polgotherick Pet Parade,' Tammy said suddenly. 'You should put Pookie in too. The judges would love him!'

'Are you sure it's not too late?' I asked.

'No, the closing date's tomorrow.'

'Oh... good,' I said, trying to sound glad.

They all agreed it was a fantastic idea.

'Three pets give us three chances of winning!' they said. It was like we were a team and if one of us won then we all did.

Sasha, Tammy and Abina thought we should get all the pets together before the pet parade.

68

They didn't just want to be matching-set friends – they wanted to have matching-set pets.

'I could bring Pookie to Peony's house tomorrow,' suggested Abina. 'He'd enjoy the walk.'

'And I could bring Heavenly Honeybun in her travel box,' said Tammy.

They all looked at me. No-one had mentioned meeting at my house on Sundays again, but it looked as if they just assumed it now.

'That would be lovely,' I said, 'but I probably should warn you, my sister's got a bit of a bug. She's being sick and everything.'

I knew they wouldn't want to risk catching something right before the Young Voices competition. 'I'm sure she'll be better by next week,' I said.

I already knew what I was going to say next week – Primrose was better but now Dad had caught it. The week after that, it could be Mum. If I kept it up for long enough they might forget all about coming to my house and just let me go to theirs.

You shouldn't lie to people, especially your friends, so I didn't feel very proud of myself. But on the other hand, I couldn't help looking forward to a normal Sunday on my own, with nothing I had to do all day except breathe in and breathe out.

Chapter 9
Mime-time with Mum and the Emergency Meeting

The good thing about Sam is he understands; the good thing about Dennis is he doesn't. You can say whatever you like to him, he won't get upset.

'I don't know why we're bothering with all this brushing,' I said, picking up the brush and flopping down on the rug. Dennis hopped over to me. I scooped him onto my lap. 'We haven't got a snowflake-in-the-desert's chance of winning now that Heavenly Honeybun and Pookie are in the competition.'

Dennis had bits of fresh hay in his fur and food on his face from his routine kicking-and-tipping the minute I had finished cleaning out his hutch.

'Who's Heavenly Honeybun?' Dad said. He had just been next door to get his problem page letters and answers from Mr Kaminski, ready for his conference call with the agony aunts. 'And who is Pookie?'

I explained, but he wasn't really listening. He was too busy fiddling with his laptop.

'Are you doing that in here?' Mum said, coming in from the yard.

'Yes, the living room's covered in the kids' mess.'

'Hey!' I protested. 'None of that stuff is mine. Blame Primrose.'

'Do you want us to go somewhere else?' Mum said. 'Only I really do need to keep an eye on my sponge.'

She was making a cake to take up to Nash House. Gran, Jane and Mr Kaminski were going up there that afternoon to strip the wallpaper in the front room and Stella was helping Mum with the garden. They used to work together at the Green Fingers Garden Centre before they set up their own business, Garden Angels.

'Shh!' said Dad. 'They're here.'

He said hello to the agony aunts. We couldn't see them this time because Dad was on the far side of the table and the screen was pointing the other way. Mum shrugged and sat down on the rug beside me.

Kay asked Dad if his friends were still teasing him and he said yes, they were. Alice tut-tutted. Jeannie hoped he was managing to keep his spirits up. You could almost hear the chin-wobble in her voice.

'We can't manage next weekend, but we've set a date for taking you out to lunch – it's going to be the Saturday after next.'

Mum waved her hand and shook her head at Dad, but he ignored her.

'That sounds lovely,' he said.

Mum jumped up. She acted out a mime of playing football. I remembered the Saturday after next was the day Dad's team were playing in the five-a-side final.

'You couldn't make it any other day?' Dad asked the agony aunts. They checked their diaries. The next date they had free was after Christmas which, they all agreed, was too long to wait. So Dad said thank you, and that he'd look forward to it.

Mum gave him a 'you're going to regret that'

look as she tiptoed across to the oven to check her cake, then tiptoed back again. It wasn't quite ready.

Dad was all right talking about his own readers' problems because he had got Mr Kaminski's answers in front of him, but he was out of his depth when the other agony aunts talked about theirs.

'I've got one here from someone called James,' said Jeannie. She read it out. 'Dear Jeannie, I've put on so much weight since the summer I can't do my trousers up any more. Please don't tell me to diet because I haven't got any will-power, and I don't like exercising...'

'If he won't diet or exercise, I don't know what you can suggest,' Kay said.

'New trousers?' goes Dad.

They laughed. 'You are funny!' they said. 'But seriously...'

Mum waved to get Dad's attention again. She grabbed me and pretended to be a doctor, listening to my lungs with her stethoscope.

'He should go and see his doctor!' said Dad.

'Yes!' goes Kay. 'He may have a medical condition that's made him put on weight.'

Mum let go of me and mimed being in floods of tears.

'Or he might be depressed!' said Dad.

With Mum's help, Dad got through the rest of the conference call without making any more bad suggestions.

'I think I'm getting the hang of this,' he said, as he closed his computer afterwards.

Mum rolled her eyes.

'What?' goes Dad.

She didn't answer. She just shook her head. Dad gathered his Dear Daphne letters into a tidy pile and tucked them into his laptop case.

'You can't go to lunch with the agony aunts the Saturday after next,' Mum said. 'You'll be letting your five-a-side team mates down.'

'They don't need me,' said Dad. 'There are seven of us and one on the bench is plenty of back-up.'

Mum looked as if she was going to argue but before she could say another word the smoke alarm went off. The noise was deafening. Dennis shot underneath his hutch. Dad grabbed the broom from the cupboard and started poking at the alarm with the handle. Mum flung open the oven door and smoke came billowing out.

Crack! Dad poked too hard and the cover fell off the smoke alarm.

Smack! Mum burnt her fingers on the hot cake tin and dropped it on the floor.

Thump! Dennis banged his back feet to warn any passing rabbits there was a flying cake hazard.

Dad gave the smoke alarm a mighty prod with the broom handle. The battery bounced out and fell to the floor in a shower of plastic splinters.

In the silence that followed, we looked down at the cake. Dad said at least it had landed right side up. Mum said that didn't make any difference – the cake was dead. 'Dead – and cremated,' agreed Dad.

After lunch, Dad went to watch Plymouth play at home and Mum and me got ready to go to Gran's. It didn't matter about the cake because Stella rang to say she was bringing a bag of doughnuts.

Primrose was upstairs with Matt, watching a DVD. If it was a mushy one, they'd be all cuddled up together and if it was a scary one she'd be glued to him like a love sick limpet. Either way, you did not want to go in there.

We were just leaving when my mobile rang. It was Sasha. She sounded in a state. Something terrible had happened, she said. Abina and Tammy had come round for an emergency meeting and now they were on their way up to my house to talk to me.

'I'm not at my house,' I said, which was technically true since Mum had just shut the front door. 'I could meet you somewhere. Are you near the harbour?'

Mum took off up to Gran's and I walked down the hill towards the harbour. Sasha, Tammy and Abina were waiting impatiently outside the Milk Bar and as soon as I got there we all went inside out of the cold. Sasha bought shakes for everyone.

'It's a disaster,' she said, bringing them across to the table. 'Abina's cousins are coming over from America.'

A disaster? What were these cousins – gun-toting gangsters?

'The problem is they can only come the day of the Young Voices competition,' Tammy explained.

'I'll have to go out for dinner with them,' Abina said.

'So she won't be able to be our Chair,' Sasha and Tammy said together.

They all looked expectantly at me.

'That's rotten luck,' I said. 'What are you going to do?'

They all looked at each other.

'We want you to do it,' said Sasha. 'You've heard my talk lots of times and watched us practise, so you know the Chairman's speech already.'

'Please say yes,' said Tammy.

'Pretty please,' said Sasha.

I didn't think Jess would mind. I mean, I was

only doing the vote of thanks for her and anyone could do that – it was just a few words at the end, nothing tricky. She would find someone else, no bother.

So I said I would do it, and they straight away jumped up and gave me a big hug, which was kind of embarrassing but also very nice.

If I was honest, it did feel good to know I was on the winners' team, and instead of giving the vote of thanks for Jess's talk about Fives I would be introducing the coolest girl in the class talking on the super-cool subject of The World of Fashion.

Plus I wouldn't have to worry about Toby turning up in shorts and everybody laughing.

Chapter 10
Jess in a Stress and the Other Garden Angel

I bumped into Jess on the way into school and told her straight away. I wanted to give her as much time as possible to find someone else.

She didn't say anything. She stopped walking and sort of stared at me.

'You don't mind do you?' I said. 'I mean, Sasha was in a panic. It's hard to get a new Chairperson at the last minute, and I already know the introduction speech because I've heard Abina do it lots of times.'

She went on staring.

'You can easily get someone else to do the vote of thanks,' I said. 'It's only a few words.'

Jess blinked, turned her back on me and walked away. What was her problem? It was just the vote of thanks. It was nothing. Anyone could do it. Maybe she had something else on her mind and it was just bad timing.

I caught up with Toby on the way into class.

'I can't do the vote of thanks now because Sasha needs a new Chair,' I said. 'I've told Jess, but she was really off with me.'

I explained about how it would be much harder to find a new Chair at the last minute than a new vote-of-thanks-person.

'There isn't even any need to practise the vote of thanks,' I said. 'You could drag someone out from the audience to do it.'

'But Jess isn't happy?' said Toby.

I held the classroom door open for him. 'I don't want to let you down but what am I supposed to do? Sasha's in a fix and she needs me more than you do.'

Toby said he would talk to Jess. He swivelled himself round on his crutches and dropped into his seat.

At break time I looked at the list outside the library to see who was already in a Young Voices team. Loads of people weren't, but by the time you crossed off all the ones who poked fun at Toby or thought Jess was a freak, that only left five.

The best of the rest was the new girl, April Grey. She was a bit shy, as in no-one had ever heard her say anything, but she was bound to speak up on the day. It would be good for her. It would bring her out of her shell and help her to make new friends.

She wasn't keen at first. She whispered something about not liking standing up in front of people and never having done any public speaking before. I said in that case, giving a vote of thanks was the perfect place to begin! It was literally just a question of saying, 'Thank you, Jess – that was a lovely speech.'

You would have thought Jess would be grateful to me for finding a new vote-of-thanks-person but oh, no. She gave me the silent treatment again when I told her, as if I had done something wrong in trying to help.

'If you'll excuse us,' she said, 'we've got a presentation to practise.'

Toby went after her, swinging off down the corridor on his crutches.

It hadn't gone the way I had expected it to. Jess never usually gets into a stress and Toby always understands. Maybe it was a problem for them after all, me having new friends. Maybe they were jealous.

Well, it wasn't my fault if they wanted to be unreasonable. I tried to forget about it, but it bugged me all day and it was still bugging me after school at Sasha's.

We had hot scones straight from the oven that Margaret had made, and watched Vampire Girl on DVD. Everyone was keen for me to practise my introduction speech, so we turned the TV off after one episode and Abina gave me her notes.

'You won't need notes on the day,' they said. 'But perhaps you should use them the first few times.'

I stood up in front of them and delivered my introduction, and they pretended to be the audience. Even with notes, I was hopeless compared with Abina.

'Could you hold your head up a bit?' suggested Sasha. 'That's better!'

'Could you maybe talk a little slower?' suggested Tammy.

'It's bound to take time,' Abina said. 'Practice makes perfect!'

We ran through it five times but I didn't seem to get any better. They kept trying to encourage me like they did with the netball. They could have told me I was rubbish but instead they said things like, 'It's nearly there!' and 'It's going to be so good!'

The problem was my heart wasn't in it, and that was Toby and Jess's fault. Why couldn't they just have been fine with me switching? Why couldn't they have been happy with April? It shouldn't be a Big Deal.

I plodded home super-slowly up the hill. I felt like one of those donkeys that have to be rescued because they're nearly dead from carrying huge heavy loads. I had Toby and Jess piling on the silent treatment and Sasha, Tammy and Abina expecting me to be brilliant like them and not let the side down.

Mum spotted I wasn't having a great day the minute I walked in.

'Woah, Peony! Why the long face?'

She and Stella were working on a garden design. They had pictures and plans spread out all over the kitchen table. I didn't really want to talk about it with Stella there but I couldn't stop myself. I opened my mouth and it all just spilled out.

I told them the whole story, everything that had happened. Somehow they managed to totally miss the point. What was wrong with everyone today?

'I'm a bit surprised you switched,' Mum said. 'I thought Jess's talk sounded really interesting.'

'What was it about?' asked Stella.

'Fives,' goes Mum. 'Jess likes the number five. That's right, isn't it, Peony?'

'Maybe Sasha's talk is even better,' suggested Stella.

'What's Sasha's about?' asked Mum.

'The World of Fashion, but that's really not important,' I snapped.

'I didn't know you were interested in fashion,' said Mum.

'Everyone's interested in fashion,' I said. 'That's why it's fashionable.'

'Yes, but I didn't know you were.'

Was I?

'That's not the point!' I said, trying not to shout. 'The point is, I was just trying to help Sasha out of a tight spot and now Jess isn't talking to me!'

They exchanged a glance.

'So, to get this straight,' Mum said, 'you told Sasha you would be her Chair, and then you told Jess you couldn't do her vote of thanks?'

'Yes.'

Finally!

'Well the problem is, you got it the wrong way round,' said Mum. 'You should really have asked Jess if she would mind before you agreed to join Sasha's team.'

'What's the difference?'

'Imagine you're Jess,' Mum said. 'Then you'll know what the difference is.'

I was so cross, I went to my room. I stretched out on my bed and looked at my wall of dogs. They might not be as cool as sports stars and supermodels but they had their uses. I started counting through them. 1, German Shepherd; 2, Border Terrier; 3, Dalmatian... By the time I'd got to 23, Golden Retriever, I was beginning to calm down.

I tried to imagine how Jess felt when I told her I couldn't do her vote of thanks, and then I imagined how she would have felt if I had asked her whether she minded first. It probably would have been better, but there still wasn't any need for her to go off on one.

When Stella left I went back downstairs to look for Dennis. Mum was tidying the table, putting the pictures and papers in a pile.

'We were talking about Gran's garden,' she said. 'Stella's got some great ideas for the area round the pond.'

I looked under Dennis's hutch. He wasn't there. I opened his door but he wasn't inside either.

'Stella knows someone who's got a gazebo for sale.'

What was a gazebo? I didn't know and I didn't

care. I looked under the table. No Dennis.

'I love talking to Stella about gardens!' sighed Mum.

Stella, Stella, Stella... Mum couldn't half go on. I found Dennis under the window, hiding behind the curtain.

'Anyone would think Stella was your best friend, not just someone you work with,' I mumbled.

Mum said Stella used to be just someone she worked with at the Green Fingers Garden Centre, but since the two of them had set up Garden Angels together she had become a real friend. In fact, that was one of the best things about setting up the business.

'But she's much older than you,' I said.

Stella's children were all grown-up. She was skinny and stringy, with creases round her eyes and a strip of white down the middle of her hair like a badger.

'That's an odd thing to say,' said Mum. 'What difference does it make how old you are if you like spending time together?'

I suddenly remembered Becky's face when she overheard me telling Sasha, Tammy and Abina she was just someone I worked with.

'Talking about ponds,' Mum said. 'Is it true you can't put fish and frogs together?'

Chapter 11
The Great Mistake and the Golden Rule

The next morning something happened that should have made everything OK. Mr Jimson called me, Sasha and Jess over to his desk and told us he'd checked the rules and we couldn't change teams once the names were in.

'You'll have to find someone who isn't already in a team to be your Chair, Sasha.'

'So that's all right,' I said to Jess. 'I can do your vote of thanks after all.'

She blanked me and later, at lunchtime, when she and Toby went off to practise, she wouldn't let me go with them.

'Like you told us,' she said sarcastically, 'the vote of thanks is sooo easy, there really isn't any need to practise.'

Toby looked unhappy but he didn't stick up for me.

Trudging home down the zig-zag path after school, I still felt like that donkey, only worse. Besides the silent treatment from Toby and Jess, I was beginning to feel bad about Becky.

When I reached the last bend before our house, I stopped to look over the stile. The sea was flat calm, not like my brain. A little way along the coastal footpath, Nash House stood looking gloomy behind its high wall.

There was a pale smudgy line like a pencil mark rising straight up from the garden. It was only a few hundred metres away, so I went to investigate. I found Gran and Jane from the Happy Haddock standing either side of a shiny new burning-bin, having an argument.

'I'm telling you, it isn't going to work!' said Jane.

'And I'm telling you it is!'

They both peered into the burning-bin, which was like a metal dustbin on feet, with little holes round the bottom. The smudgy line of smoke streamed up into the air from somewhere deep inside it.

Gran glanced up and, catching sight of me, said, 'What do you think, Peony?'

I picked my way between a heap of fallen leaves gathered up ready for burning and a mountain of branches Mum and Stella had cut down when they were clearing the garden on Sunday.

'Don't put your granddaughter in a tight spot like that,' Jane said to Gran. 'Anyone can see this fire is a non-starter.'

Gran stuck her garden fork into the burning-bin and hauled out a big bunch of smoky sticks and leaves.

'Nonsense,' she said. 'You just put too much in. You were deliberately trying to put it out!'

Jane rolled her eyes.

'Your gran and her great ideas,' she said. 'You know what this reminds me of?'

'That was your fault too,' said Gran. 'It would have worked fine if you'd done it properly.'

'What?' I asked. 'What are you talking about?'

They both turned to look at me, as if they'd momentarily forgotten I was there.

'When your gran and I were at school, we found a box of matches in the playground.'

'All the teachers smoked in those days,' Gran said. 'It probably fell out of one of their pockets.'

'I wanted to hand it in,' said Jane. 'Only madam here had a better idea. "Let's do smoke signals like cowboys and Indians," she says.'

'All the films were about cowboys and Indians when we were young,' said Gran.

'We went into the gap behind the play-sheds, where lots of leaves had got blown, and we pulled them into a heap. It was a warm dry day, not a damp drizzly one like today. If it had been a day like today we'd have been fine, because nothing's going to burn on a day like this, is it?'

Gran muttered something. Jane took no notice.

'So we strike a match and put it under the leaves, and they start to smoulder, little bits of smoke at first, and then a steady stream. Your gran says, "Use your sweater to make the signals. Lay it over to stop the smoke, then pull it away. I'll go to the other side of the playground and count the puffs." I think you can guess what happened next.'

'You were only supposed to lay your sweater over it for a second,' Gran said.

'I did, but it happened to be the second the flames broke through, and it was bye-bye school sweater, hello Headmaster's Office.'

'I got detention too.'

'Yes, but you didn't ruin your sweater. I got grounded for a fortnight because of that.'

'Getting grounded wasn't really too much of a punishment for you though, was it?' Gran said.

'Not really,' agreed Jane. 'Living in the sticks doesn't do much for someone's social life.'

They suddenly stopped arguing and laughed, remembering.

'So you didn't go round each other's houses after school?' I said.

'I couldn't,' Jane said. 'We didn't have a car, and anyway, there's only so much of your gran's good ideas a person can take!'

'And I didn't really want to,' said Gran. 'I was never that sociable as a girl. I liked messing around on my own.'

'I'm like that,' I said, without even thinking about it.

As soon as the words came out, I saw that it was true. I liked seeing Becky at the kennels and doing outdoors things with Toby; I liked talking about interesting stuff with Jess. But I also liked lying around reading, or watching David Attenborough, or finding new dogs for my wall. I liked talking to Sam and playing with Dennis.

That's when I saw my great mistake. I had thought I wanted to be friends with Sasha, Tammy and Abina because everyone did. They were the coolest girls in class; they were clever and nice. But they wanted to do everything together – and they were wearing me out!

The thing was, everybody was different, and that meant they wanted different kinds of friends. Matching-set friends were great for sociable people like Sasha, Tammy and Abina. But interesting friends who weren't too demanding, like Becky, Toby and Jess... they were the perfect friends for me.

Except I'd really upset them.

'Are you alright, Peony?' Gran said. 'You look like you've seen a ghost.'

'It was probably the ghost of this dead bonfire,' said Jane.

'All it needs is some firelighters.'

I walked down to the shop to get some firelighters for Gran. Things were a mess, friends wise, but at least I knew what I wanted now. Mr Kaminski says knowing what you want is the first step to getting it. He says you have to know exactly what you want, and write it down – that's the golden rule.

When you've written it down, you think about it and think about until ideas start to come. Then you try one idea and another and another, until you find one that works.

So when I got home I found some paper and wrote it down:

I want to be friends again with Toby, Jess and Becky, and I want to stop being part of Sasha's set.

Chapter 12

Four Facts about Friends and Making Amends

I slept with my wish list under my pillow and when I woke up in the morning I had some good ideas about what to do. That's the magic of Mr Kaminski's method.

When it came to Becky, Toby and Jess, I had to say sorry and make amends. That's what Mum told Primrose to do when she dumped Matt because someone showed her a pic of him giving another girl a hug, and it turned out she was his cousin. I wasn't sure how to do the amends bit, but I could certainly start straight away with saying sorry.

When it came to Sasha, Tammy and Abina, the best thing would be to ease myself out gradually, making excuses for not going round their houses until they stopped inviting me.

But when I tried to say sorry to Jess and Toby they kept avoiding me, and when I finally caught up with them at break time, Jess cut me off in the middle of my sentence.

'Shall I tell you Five Fascinating Facts about Friends? One – they stick together. Two – they aren't embarrassed about each other...'

I felt my face go hot. I didn't think anyone else knew how I secretly felt about Toby's shorts, Jess's unusual ideas and Becky's charity-shop clothes.

'Three – they don't let each other down. Four – if they do mess up, they're sorry...'

'But that's what I'm trying to say,' I butted in. 'I am sorry.'

'If you're sorry it's just because you aren't in Sasha's team any more and therefore you aren't going to win.'

She turned and walked off. I felt confused. She was normally so easy-going, but suddenly it was like she'd taken strop-lessons from Primrose.

'She's really upset,' Toby said, with a shrug. He limped off after her. He wasn't using the crutches any more, but it didn't look as if his ankle was completely better.

'That's only four facts about friends!' I called after them, but they didn't even look back.

So far, so bad, and things didn't go any better with Sasha, Tammy and Abina. When I told them I couldn't go to Tammy's after school they thought I was upset because their new Chair, Olivia Wyre, was coming.

'She's only coming because we need to practise with her,' Sasha said. 'We'd much rather have you on our team.'

'You can do it next year,' Abina said. 'One of us will stand down.'

'Anyway,' said Tammy, 'you've got to come this afternoon to help with Heavenly Honeybun. We're going to get her used to being handled for the pet parade, and you're the expert. We need you!'

They wouldn't take no for an answer, so we all went to Tammy's after school, Sasha, Tammy, Abina, Olivia and me. Abina and I watched the others doing their Young Voices practice and we all said well done to Olivia and told her how good she was.

After they had run through it several times, we went down to the bottom of the garden to see Heavenly Honeybun. We fed her some grass through the mesh on her door while Tammy put on the gardening gloves. As soon as Heavenly Honeybun saw them, she bolted into the bedroom end of her hutch and thumped her feet furiously on the wooden floor.

Tammy very slowly opened the hutch. Heavenly Honeybun glared at her in a 'just you dare' kind of way. After one or two half-hearted tries it became clear that Tammy didn't really dare, even in the thick leather gloves, so she stood back and looked at me.

I put on the gloves and offered my hand low to the floor of the hutch so that Heavenly Honeybun could push her nose under it. She tried to bite me. One thing was for sure, she wasn't at all like Dennis.

I made a grab for her and lifted her, kicking and wriggling, out of the hutch. I sat down and put her on the shed floor beside me, keeping one hand over her face until she calmed down.

Sasha, Tammy, Abina and Olivia were impressed. 'How did you do that?' they said. Tammy fetched Heavenly Honeybun's brush and they took turns brushing her sides while I held her.

'You're so good with animals,' said Abina. 'I can't wait for you to help me put Pookie through his paces.'

I said I was really sorry but I wouldn't be able to go to her house on Saturday.

'My friend Becky from the kennels is running a stall for the RSPCA at the pet parade,' I told them. 'I promised her I'd help. She's doing a tombola and stuff.'

They seemed genuinely disappointed, but they said they understood. Sasha asked if Becky had plenty of prizes because if she didn't she was sure her mum would donate something from the shop. Abina said she could get her parents to give something too, and Tammy went to ask her mum straight away.

A few minutes later, she came back with a brand new bird-feeder.

'Mum bought this yesterday but she says she can easily buy another one. She's going to ask her friends to make a donation too. This is going to be the best tombola ever!'

By the time I saw Becky on Saturday morning I had two big bags of prizes from Sasha, Tammy and Abina's parents and their friends. That was some serious amends!

But saying sorry was difficult because Becky seemed completely normal with me, as if she'd never overheard me saying that she wasn't my friend. But I knew she had. I remembered the hurt look on her face.

All morning, as we cleaned out the pens and walked the dogs, I was trying to find the right moment to tell her I was sorry for saying what I said, but there wasn't really a chance.

I went into the farmhouse to see Sam while Becky was finishing up. It was lovely being able to hang around longer and not be in a rush because of going to Abina's. Sam seemed to think it didn't matter too much about saying sorry. 'She knows you didn't mean it,' he seemed to say.

'I did mean it, though.'

'All right then, she knows you were just being stupid.'

Harsh but true, Sam.

After lunch we laid all the prizes out on Becky's kitchen table. It was completely crammed. Half of them were normal tombola prizes such as tins of peaches and supermarket shower gel, but the rest were much too good for a tombola, where every 50p ticket wins. There were expensive glossy books and arty picture frames and vouchers for free facials at Beachside Beauty. There was a hamper from Healthy Ways and a gift box from the chocolate shop.

We decided to split the prizes into two sections and run a raffle as well as a tombola.

When we had organised everything for Becky's stall we went to my house to do a practice with

Dennis. I picked him up and put him on the table, like they do in the pet parade, and Becky pretended to be the judge.

Dennis got a bit edgy when Becky stroked him and I thought he might bolt, so I rested my finger gently across his nose, and he settled again. I explained how he would sit still for hours, quite happily, as long as he had his nose underneath something. That was his rabbit nature.

Becky took a penny out of her pocket.

'Would it work with this?'

I shrugged. I didn't think so. Really I meant he liked to put his nose under a hand or foot, not have something light and small balancing on it.

Becky gently placed the penny on Dennis's nose. He sat completely still until she took it off again. I put him on the floor and gave him a bit of cream cracker. He munched it up and then licked up all the bits, getting crumbs all over his whiskers.

'That is one happy bunny,' said Becky. 'He deserves to win first prize.'

'Being happy won't be enough against a beautiful pet like Heavenly Honeybun or one that's clever and well-trained like Pookie,' I said.

'Well, it should be,' said Becky.

I had some pictures of pot-bellied pigs and Blue French Angora rabbits in my book of unusual pets so we went upstairs to look for it. First stop, the living room. Primrose's duvet was still draped over the settee from her Saturday morning TV-fest and there was a snow-storm of tissues on the floor – she must have been watching something mushy.

Next stop, my bedroom. The super-size mug Matt gave me with the photo of Sam on it had a crust of last night's hot milk round the inside and my tiger bedspread was all crumpled up in the corner of my bed, with my wish list poking out from under it.

I whisked it into my pocket and as I did so – more wish-magic – I suddenly knew how to break friends with Sasha, Tammy and Abina without upsetting them.

As soon as Becky went, I phoned Sasha.

'As I couldn't come to Abina's today,' I said, 'I was wondering if you would all like to come to my house tomorrow?'

Chapter 13
The Tick-list of Fear and the Normal Sunday

When I wanted to be friends forever with Sasha, Tammy and Abina, there was a list of things I was scared might happen if they came to my house:

1 Mum cooking anything except frozen pizza
2 Dad saying something mad and meaning it
3 Primrose being a drama queen
4 The house looking as if an earthquake had hit it – which it mostly had, that earthquake being Primrose.

If I still wanted to be friends and they were coming to my house, there was a list of actions I would have to take to try and stop these things from happening:

1 Hide the vegetables
2 Make sure Dad wasn't around
3 Make sure Matt was
4 Do the housework myself – it's no good waiting for Mum to do it because she's always busy with the business, and Dad's motto is 'Nature abhors a vacuum cleaner'.

Sasha, Tammy and Abina all had neat, tidy houses and non-embarrassing families. Even their pets were tidily outside. They were organised and calm; they probably never got in the kind of state I'd have been in if I still wanted to be friends and everything kicked off just before they were about to arrive. But I didn't want to stay friends forever, so I let it wash over me.

Sasha, Tammy and Abina were coming at two o'clock and we didn't start lunch until half past one. As it happened, Mum had cooked frozen pizza, but she'd also boiled up a vat of sprouts to go with it, and even a handful of sprouts will make your house smell like something's died in your drains.

Dad had been holding out all week to talk to

the agony aunts because he was fed up with his footie friends not having any people skills. They were still teasing him and calling him Daphne, but now they were also annoyed with him for dropping out of the five-a-side.

However, when he did his conference call, the agony aunts kept laughing at him because they thought he was joking when he wasn't.

'They said honesty was the best policy when we were talking about Jeannie's letter from Guilty of Gossington, who was wondering whether to tell his girlfriend he'd gone off her, but when we finished talking about the letters and Kay asked us if we liked her new hair colour...'

'Oh, dear – you didn't,' sighed Mum.

'Well, pardon me for having a point of view, but purple was bad enough – blue-black makes her look like a witch in a wig.'

Primrose was texting under the table and refusing to eat her sprouts so Mum was getting wound up with her, but Primrose didn't care. She was away with the love-fairies, all gooey-eyed, like she always is when she's texting with Matt.

'He says we should have a special celebration for our six-month anniversary,' she said. 'We're going to wear the same clothes and go for a walk on the cliff path, just like the first time we went out.'

That's dating, Polgotherick-style.

'Six months isn't till after Christmas,' said Mum.

'You probably won't even still be going out with him,' said Dad.

Primrose gave a strangled squeal and stood up, scraping her chair across the floor. She's got super-sonic emotions; she can go from gooey-eyed to wild-eyed in under two seconds.

'How could you say that?'

She stormed out of the room, slamming the door behind her. We heard her footsteps stamping away up the stairs.

'What?' goes Dad. 'It's true!'

'Just because something's true, that doesn't mean you have to say it,' said Mum.

Dad normally does the dishes on a Sunday but he got in a huff and said he was late for his match. He looked for his notepad and voice-recorder, muttering away to himself that at least you knew where you were with work and you also knew where you were with sport.

'Someone scores a great goal, you tell it like it is. Someone plays like a hippo with a headache, you tell it like it is...'

'Can you do the dishes then, Peony?' said Mum.

'Sorry, but not really – I've still got to clean out Dennis before my friends arrive.'

I opened both the doors of his hutch and fetched a black bag and a brush. Dennis got all territorial. He crouched behind his food bowl ready to pounce.

Mum gathered the dirty plates noisily and dumped them in the sink. She turned the taps on so hard the water sprayed all over the place like a fountain in a force nine gale.

Right then, there was a rat-a-tat-tat on the front door. Dennis thumped hard with his back feet, making his hutch floor rattle like a drum. Dad was nearest the door, so he opened it, just in time for Sasha, Tammy and Abina to hear the ear-splitting scream that suddenly erupted from Primrose's bedroom.

Dennis thumped again. Primrose started to wail. I read in Amazing Animals of the World that a lion's roar can carry up to five miles away, which sounds impressive until you hear what Primrose can do.

Mum grabbed a tea-towel and disappeared up the stairs to try and stop her from waking up the Australians. The sudden movement spooked Dennis. He burst out of his hutch and shot round the room, making Sasha, Tammy and Abina spill back onto the doorstep.

Dad said, 'It was lovely meeting you, girls,' as he edged past to go to his match. Then he remarked on what nice shoes they were wearing, looking back at me in a smug way as if to say, 'See, I can do it if I want to!'

I jumped up and got to the door just in time to stop Dennis from disappearing down the front steps. I scooped him up and ushered Sasha, Tammy and Abina back inside.

We heard Mum's voice upstairs saying something soothing and then Primrose screamed, 'Go away, Mum! You aren't helping!' Mum didn't go away, but went on trying to talk her down, which only made her wail again.

'Do you mind if I finish cleaning out Dennis?' I said to Sasha, Tammy and Abina.

They sat round the half-cleared kitchen table, watching while I wrestled the old newspaper out of Dennis's hutch and tried to sweep up the old hay, with him tugging at the brush. I didn't do that nose-under-hand thing so I knew it would get messy.

I managed to get the paper and hay into the black bag, and then Dennis abandoned ship and dived in after it, kicking around furiously in it, making bits fly back out.

'He's very lively,' Sasha said, picking up a stray sprout and popping it back in the bowl.

'He's sweet,' said Abina.

Primrose yelled again and Dennis did one of

his dashes. Tammy only just lifted her feet up in time.

I lined Dennis's hutch with fresh paper, put the hay in the bedroom end and gave him fresh food and water. He arrived back from his dash just as I finished, jumped up into his hutch, grabbed the food bowl in his teeth and tipped it over.

'All done!' I said, cheerfully. 'Would you like to see round the house?'

As we went up the first flight of stairs we could hear what Primrose and Mum were saying.

'Happiness has made me fat!' Primrose wailed.

'But most of your clothes fit fine,' Mum said.

'He wants me to wear the dress I was wearing on The Day!'

'He won't care what you wear. What about this yellow one?'

'Noooooooooooooo!'

As we went up the second flight to Primrose and my bedrooms we saw clothes strewn over the landing and, looking in at her door, Mum sitting on the bed amongst a heap of clothes, trying to stay calm and reasonable.

'Primrose darling, he loves you. Even if you have put on a little, teeny, tiny bit of weight...'

'Ohhhhhhhhhhhhh!'

Mum mouthed, 'Hello,' to Sasha, Tammy and Abina – or she might have said it out loud, but we couldn't hear her. We went into my bedroom and closed the door.

'Wow – you really do like dogs!' Tammy said.

'And you've got so many books about animals,' goes Sasha.

We had a look through some of my books and they seemed really interested, especially when I showed them the sections on pot-bellied pigs and fancy rabbits in the one about unusual pets.

The noise was quite loud in my bedroom and Primrose can keep it up for hours, so I suggested we went back downstairs. When I opened the door we were hit by a wall of sound as Primrose yelled, 'He's going to dump me – I know he is! I might as well finish with him now and get it over with!'

We sat around trying to watch TV for a while, and then Mum came through on her way back down to the kitchen. She said Matt was coming over later.

What she meant was that it would soon be over. Primrose would wash her face and put on some make-up, find a baggy sweater to hide in and melt into Matt's arms.

Mum didn't stop to chat – you never feel like talking when you've been Primrosed. You feel like moving to the Antarctic and living with the seals.

'Hmm...' I said, when she had gone. 'This might not be pretty.'

'Are they going to have a big row, do you think?' said Sasha. 'Is she going to dump him?'

'I don't know,' I shrugged.

'Perhaps it would be better if we weren't here when he comes.'

We played on the PlayStation after that, with the sound of Mum tidying up in the kitchen coming up from downstairs and Primrose flinging stuff around in her bedroom above.

'We don't seem to have come on a very good day,' Tammy said later, as they were leaving.

'Oh, it's just the normal Sunday,' I said. 'Next week, you could come for lunch if you like.'

'You'd be most welcome,' Mum said. 'There's always plenty to eat if you like winter veg!'

The chance of Sasha, Tammy and Abina wanting to come again was about the same as the chance of Primrose and Matt making it to their six-month anniversary.

It felt a bit sad but in a way, it really couldn't have gone better.

Chapter 14
Young Voices and the
Fifth Fact about Friends

I didn't go to Sasha's after school on Monday or Tammy's on Wednesday because they were practising their Young Voices and I said I was too. They probably thought I was practising with my team, but the truth was Toby and Jess hadn't invited me and I didn't want to keep asking.

I was practising though, just on my own. I wrote my speech and re-wrote it, until it was the best I could make it, and then I learned it by heart, like Sasha and her team, until I got it perfect.

It was the Cornish regional final and the two top teams would be going on from there to the South West final in Bristol. When Mum and Dad and me arrived at the hall, it was already filling up.

The teams had their own section of seating on one side at the front, and the judges' chairs were in the middle, behind a long table.

Mum and Dad went to find some seats and I took my place with Toby and Jess. We were in the row behind Sasha, Tammy and Olivia, and they turned round to wish us good luck. Everyone was very excited.

Looking around the hall I saw Mum and Dad sitting near the back and a few rows down from them, Toby's mum and dad with his little sister, Leah. Jess's mum was close to the front but I couldn't see her dad, so maybe he had to work late that night.

By the time the judges filed in, the hall was packed. The first teams to go up were from Truro, Penzance and St Ives, and then it was Sasha's turn. Her team looked perfect up there on the stage, a perfect matching set of school uniforms and tidy, tied-back hair.

Their speeches were perfect too. They stuck to the correct timings for each part, even the bit where the Chair takes questions from the audience, which is tricky to time. They were so going to win.

We had to go straight on after them. Toby was in shorts but at least they were proper grey ones, so it looked as if he was wearing school uniform from the knees up. Jess didn't normally wear uniform to school – no-one knew how she got away with it, but she had her own versions of blue tops over grey skirts or trousers. So she'd had to borrow a school sweatshirt, and it was a bit too big. I was wearing my best school uniform because I wanted to do my best for Toby and Jess.

As we went up on stage, I caught sight of Jess's dad at the back of the hall. He must have arrived too late to get a place next to her mum. The head judge jotted something on his notepad and then nodded to us to begin.

I hadn't heard Toby's introduction before but it was really good. He was confident and funny, and he made us look forward to hearing Jess's talk.

Jess was a bit shy to start with, but she soon warmed up.

After she had given us her five facts about the Young Voices competition, she told us about how she first began to love fives at playgroup. I remembered it! She used to build with five bricks and paint with five colours, everything five.

Jess explained that the picture on the big screen behind us that she had chosen to illustrate her talk was of the five trees in her garden, which were the reason why her house was called Five Trees. She showed us her notebook and read some of her lists.

Toby over-ran a bit on the question-and-answer session because he wanted to take five questions.

Then it was my turn. My legs suddenly turned to jelly. I wasn't worried about the audience; I was worried about Toby and Jess. They had no idea what I was going to say, and I had no idea what they would think of it.

I took a deep breath. 'Thank you, Jess for a really wonderful talk...'

I went on to say that her talk was just like her. It was clever, and she was clever, because every time she was curious about something she went and found out about it.

It was educational, and so was being around Jess. Not many of us would have known five facts about walruses before her talk, or five facts about yogurt or Jupiter or oak trees.

I said Jess's talk was surprising, and so was she. 'I bet you weren't expecting to hear a talk like that tonight,' I said. 'You never know what to expect with Jess, and that means she's never boring or dull.'

I said Jess's talk was different, and Jess herself was different. I had never met anyone like her. 'Some people don't like that,' I said. 'But that's why I'm so happy she's my friend.'

We got a huge round of applause, the best so far, and it wasn't just because our parents were the noisiest, although Dad did forget for a moment that he wasn't at a football match and let out an ear-piercing whistle.

'You were really good!' Sasha, Tammy and Olivia said when we went back to our seats.

After all the talks were finished, the judges went off to discuss their decision. There was tea and coffee in the entrance hall for the audience and the teams went into a side-room for squash and biscuits.

I didn't know if Jess and Toby would want me to stand with them, but they came straight over to me.

'That was a lovely vote of thanks,' Jess said. 'I wanted to say, the fifth fact about friends? They forgive each other.'

I nearly fell down with relief.

'I didn't know if you would ever forgive me for letting you down like that.'

'Not you,' Jess said. 'Me. Can you forgive me?

You explained why you did it and you were right
– it would have been easier for us to find a new
vote of thanks than for Sasha to find a new Chair.'

I gawped at her.

'But I really over-reacted,' she said. 'I got into
a state and then I just couldn't seem to stop it. It
wasn't really anything to do with you, though. It
was... stuff at home.'

So that was why her mum was at the front of
the hall and her dad on his own at the back.

'I wish you had told me,' I said, but I straight
away knew she couldn't have done. Mums and
dads can be confusing and Jess hates saying
anything until she's sure of the facts.

The bell went for us to go back in. This time,
the judges were up on the stage. They went
through all the talks, saying what they liked about
each one. 'But there can only be one winner and
one runner-up going through to the Southwest
regional final next month...'

'And the winner tonight is Sasha Jones and her
team, talking about the World of Fashion!'

No surprises there, then. Sasha, Tammy and
Olivia went up to get their medals. They stayed
on the stage while the runner-up was announced.

'And the runner-up, from Truro, is Joe Davy
and his team, for their talk on Surfing.'

They went up to collect their medals too.

As the winning teams came back down off the stage, the head judge said, 'This has never happened before in the twelve years that the Young Voices competition has been running, but we feel we really must single out a third team for a special mention.'

That team was us! The judge asked us to stand up in our seats so that everyone could see us. He said we had been excellent and engaging speakers, all three of us; we were obviously the audience's favourite and it was a shame they couldn't place us in the top two, but we hadn't stuck closely enough to the rules of the competition.

'With a little more attention to detail, particularly making sure you all wear full school uniform and stick to the correct timings, we feel sure you can be a winning team next year.'

The audience gave us another loud round of applause. This time, Dad managed not to whistle.

Sasha, Tammy and Olivia said well done, and I knew they meant it because they were ever so nice. But there was also something just a little bit smug about the way they said it, as if what they really meant was, 'You're obviously not as good as us, but you tried!'

It got me thinking. Just because Sasha, Tammy and Abina had won everything for as long as anyone could remember – the best parts in school plays, the first teams in sports, the top marks in tests – that didn't mean that no-one else would ever be able to beat them. With a bit of attention to detail, with a bit of belief that it could happen, there was no reason someone else couldn't come out on top.

Maybe I had been wrong to give up on Dennis's chances in the Polgotherick Pet Parade just because Tammy and Abina had decided to enter. How amazing would it be if plain little Dennis could beat the beautiful Heavenly Honeybun and the perfectly-trained Pookie?

How good would it feel to go up against Sasha, Tammy and Abina, and take home first prize!

Chapter 15
Truffles on Trees
and Buzzy Bees

I love being in the car at night, moving through the darkness. I like the steady noise of the engine, the soft lights on the dashboard, the warm air folding round you like a soft feather quilt. I love the way the lights from passing cars sweep across the roof like searchlights and move on.

I especially like being in the car at night when Primrose isn't there, because then you know it will be peaceful, without any problems and dramas. So I was looking forward to the drive home after the competition.

As we drove through the streets of Truro, Mum, Dad and me talked about the speeches and gave them our own marks out of ten. But as we left the street-lights behind and plunged into the darkness of the open road, I settled back in my seat and dozed.

When I woke up they were talking about Dad's lunch with the agony aunts the next day.

'You don't sound very keen,' Mum said. 'I would have thought you'd be looking forward to it.'

Dad sighed.

'I don't know, Jan. It's bad enough doing the conference calls – how am I going to cope face-to-face over lunch? I try really hard but I still seem to keep saying the wrong thing. Let's face it, I'm just a bloke who likes football. I'm a fish out of water with feelings.'

Finally, Dad was having a reality check, after letting himself get carried away by being Agony Aunt of the Year.

'Maybe you should come clean with them,' suggested Mum. 'Tell them it's really Mr Kaminski who does the problem page.'

'If I do that they won't want to be friends any more.'

'Are they really the best kind of friends for you, if the idea of having lunch with them makes you feel so stressed out?'

Dad didn't say anything for a while. We turned off the main road into the lanes. Now there weren't even any passing cars, just us, gliding through the night like a spaceship moving through space.

'I can't tell them Mr Kaminski does it because I promised him I wouldn't tell anyone,' Dad said.

'Then how about just telling them someone else does it for you, and not saying who?'

There was a long silence then, until we slowed down and pulled into our usual parking-place on the top road.

'I suppose that could work,' goes Dad, switching off the engine. He sounded as keen as a lion with a lettuce.

'What choice have you got?' Mum said.

'They're going to hate me,' said Dad.

That night, I lay in bed imagining I was still in the car, with the hum of the engine, and the warm air enveloping me, and the occasional sweep of headlights from other cars driving past.

I smiled, remembering the Young Voices competition, our talk, Jess's fifth fact about friends, the judges' special mention, the audience's loud applause. Then I remembered the thought I had because of what the judges said – that Sasha, Tammy and Abina might not always be unbeatable, and maybe I'd been too quick to give up on Dennis's chances in the pet parade.

I couldn't see how he was going to win against Heavenly Honeybun and Pookie, but I knew how to get some ideas. I flicked the light on and jotted down my wish.

I want Dennis to win first prize in the Polgotherick Pet Parade.

I slid the paper under my pillow, switched off the light and fell fast asleep.

Normally, I'm the first one up on Saturday mornings but when I woke up someone was already moving around downstairs. I put my dressing gown on and went to investigate.

'Morning, Peony!' Dad greeted me cheerily as I went into the kitchen. I blinked, but he was still there.

"S going on, Dad?'

'I'm going to the five-a-side competition.'

'What about your lunch with the agony aunts?'

'It's only five minutes down the road from the sports hall – I'll pop along in the lunchbreak.'

'But that won't give you very long.'

'I don't think the agony aunts will want me for very long when they find out I'm a fraud.'

'Yeah, but...' I flopped down on the rug in front

of the radiator. Dennis hopped over to say hello. 'Doesn't that mean you're going to have a really hectic day?'

Dad doesn't usually like doing things full-on for a whole day. Mum says he needs at least one good long session of slobbing around to break things up, although he prefers to call it 'thinking time'.

'Pigs might fly if truffles grew on trees,' Dad said, handing me a glass of orange juice. I think that means, even people who like a lot of 'thinking time' will make an extra effort if the rewards are worth it.

'Have you told your football friends you're going?' I asked.

He shook his head. 'I thought it would be better to just turn up.'

It seemed to me that there were quite a few reasons why that might not be a good idea but he had made up his mind and I had other things to think about. The pet parade was the next day and I still hadn't any idea how to help Dennis win it.

I racked my brains all the way up to Becky's house and we talked about it all the way from there to the kennels. I pondered as I cleaned out the pens and walked the dogs. I talked to Sam about it.

I still didn't have any good ideas when we went back to Becky's for lunch, and by the time I left her to make the final preparations for her stall, I had given up.

The only thing Dennis had going for him was that he was a happy, healthy rabbit, and that would have to see him through. There was nothing to be done now, except a good grooming session when I got home.

When I walked in, Mum was having an argument with Primrose about not eating breakfast or lunch.

'I'm not hungry,' Primrose said.

'You weren't hungry yesterday either,' goes Mum. 'I know what you're doing, and it's very, very silly.'

'You would say that. You don't look like a big fat lump of flob.'

Dennis was hiding under his hutch and I didn't blame him. I thought I would let him lie low till things quietened down and brush him in peace later. But we were just getting to the bit when Primrose screams that no-one understands and slams out, when Gran arrived.

'I've had this great idea for Nash House,' she announced. 'It's the perfect place for a tea room!'

'Oh, Gwen,' Mum groaned. 'Have you forgotten what happened when you turned your last place into a B and B? Anyway, now you're here, help me talk some sense into your granddaughter. She's determined to starve herself!'

Rat-a-tat! Primrose opened the door to Mr Kaminski.

'I haf Daphne letters for Dave,' he said. 'Gwen! I am not knowing you are here.'

'Mr K, tell my daughter-in-law what a good idea it is for me to have a tea room in Nash House.'

'But we are haffing boat trips, no?' said Mr Kaminski, in confusion.

We obviously weren't going to get some peace any time soon, so I decided to do Dennis's grooming session anyway. It would be good practice for him keeping calm in the middle of lots of noisy people.

I got the brush and sat down on the rug, and Dennis crept over to me, keeping a low profile like a spy on a secret mission. He slid up onto my lap and I started brushing him. No-one took any notice of us. Different arguments flew in all directions like buzzy bees in a bottle.

Over the last few weeks, Dennis had got really used to being brushed and he loved it. He closed his eyes, which it says in my book that rabbits hardly ever do, because they're prey animals and if they go to sleep in the open something might come along and eat them.

Even when Dad walked in all full of himself, crying, 'Mission accomplished!' Dennis hardly budged. He pricked one ear up and then dropped it down again. That's how relaxed he was.

'The guys were a man down after the first match because Jay put his back out again,' Dad told us. 'They were pretty glad to see me. "Come on then, Daphne," they said. We finished fourth, which was better than last year.'

'And the agony aunts?' said Mum.

'They were really nice about it. They said everyone makes mistakes and leading people up the garden path probably did count as one – but the point was I came clean in the end, and that was what mattered.'

Mr Kaminski looked worried. 'You haf told them I am writing problem page?'

Dad reassured him that he hadn't told them any such thing. He had merely said a friend was writing it for him.

'And the best thing is, I haven't even blown my cover, Mr K. It turns out agony aunts have a Code of Silence and they never pass anything on. So there won't be any questions asked and everyone else will still think Daphne is me.'

'Is good,' said Mr Kaminski. 'I am not liking lemon-light.'

'Limelight,' Gran corrected him.

Dad went to have a shower, Gran and Mr Kaminski took the problem page letters upstairs to the sitting-room to go through his grammar, Primrose flounced off to her bedroom, and Mum followed to try and talk some sense into her.

I stopped brushing Dennis and put him down on the rug. He was a star, staying calm and still like that. He deserved a reward. I found his bag of rabbit treats and took one out. It looked like a chocolate button.

I was just holding it out to him when suddenly I got an idea. If I were to place it gently on his nose like Becky did with the penny, would he stay still and not eat it?

Now, that would be a very impressive trick!

Chapter 16
Mrs Mayhew-Carter's Suit and Rory MacAteer's Finger

Mum had said she would buy a travel box for Dennis to take him to the pet parade, but what with running the business and doing Gran's garden and having to cook all those winter vegetables, she forgot.

'I feel terrible,' she said. 'How are you going to manage? I can't even find a cardboard box.'

'I'll carry him. It's not far. He'll prefer it anyway.'

I held him against my shoulder with one hand and wrapped my fleecy scarf round him with the other. He was used to living indoors in the warm and it says in You and Your Rabbit that rabbits can catch a chill if you aren't careful.

Dennis's whiskers were in overdrive as we walked up the zig-zag path and both his ears were up. Mum was hovering round him like a clucky hen, worried her chick might run away. Dad, Matt and Primrose brought up the rear.

It was the first year Sam hadn't been in the pet parade, which felt a bit sad, but Matt's little brother was entering their other dog, Dasher. She was a liver-and-white Spaniel and completely nuts – her name said it all.

We arrived at the same time as Gran and Jane, who had walked up from the Happy Haddock together. As we were going in we heard a shout and turned to see Mr Kaminski huffing towards us.

Becky's stall was in a prime spot just inside the door, and she had a queue of people waiting to buy raffle tickets. Her mum was helping on the tombola and her dad was handing out leaflets and freebies, and chatting to people about the RSPCA.

There was a great long trestle table all the way down one side for the pets and a show table at the far end in front of the stage. There was a rope barrier to keep people a few feet back from the pets so they wouldn't be upset by everyone crowding round.

The long pet table was divided into sections with the cats first, then small pets, then unusual pets. There was an area cordoned off on the other side of the hall for dogs – you couldn't expect them to sit in cages and travel boxes.

Dennis's space was number 14, between a noisy white floor-mop of a guinea pig and Heavenly Honeybun. I couldn't put him down because he didn't have a box.

Sasha, Tammy and Abina said he was cute, though they obviously meant cute for a non-fancy rabbit. Heavenly Honeybun, all fluffed-up and gorgeous in her pink travel box, gave Dennis a super-snooty look.

'Where's Pookie?' I said.

He was tethered to a coat-hook at the end of the hall, all on his own. The organisers had told Abina she couldn't tie his lead to the table leg next to his space because the table wasn't heavy enough to hold him if he got boisterous.

'I told them he's properly trained, he won't get boisterous,' Abina said. 'Honestly, don't they realise that pigs are the fourth cleverest animal in the world?'

Pookie sat down without anyone even asking him to, as if to say, See how clever I am! His skin looked shiny under his bristles, and his beady eyes were bright and alert.

'Who's a pretty boy?' said Mrs Bolitho's parrot from its tall cage in the middle of the unusual pets. I didn't think he sounded quite as confident as usual.

Me and Dennis walked the whole length of the pets table. There were seven different kinds of cat, several guinea pigs and rats, six rabbits, some hamsters and gerbils, a ferret, a chinchilla, a budgie and a parrot, two snakes, a tarantula, a big lizard and lots more, all lined up in their cages, tanks and boxes.

Matt called me over to say hello to Dasher in the dogs' corner. Dennis wasn't at all bothered, even though some of those dogs would have had him for dinner.

He might jump and thump at sudden noises such as a knock on the door, he might do mad dashes and get territorial about his hutch, but he definitely wasn't scared of dogs, he was so used to Sam.

He wasn't scared of people milling around and being noisy either. Well, he wouldn't be – there was plenty of that at home.

When I took him back to Space 14 and put him on the table, he sat there quite happily watching the world go by. I did keep one hand around his chest and stroke him with the other one though, just in case something should spook him.

There were five prizes to be won – Best Dog, Best Cat, Best Small Pet, Best Unusual Pet and the top prize, Best in Show. It was obvious that Pookie would win Best Unusual Pet because he was up against spiders and snakes and stuff, and they couldn't do tricks like sitting down or lying down when their owner gave the order. The only other pet in his category that could do anything interesting was Mrs Bolitho's parrot, and he was looking even tattier than last year.

Heavenly Honeybun was definitely the most beautiful pet in the small pets section, but Dennis might be in with a chance if she won Best in Show because then Best Small Pet would still be up for grabs.

Toby's little sister Leah came to say hello, with Toby and Jess close behind. They had a good luck card for Dennis. When I showed it to him he grabbed it in his teeth and started to nibble the corner.

'He's going to need all the luck he can get,' I said, taking it off him.

There was a sudden hush in the hall and everyone turned expectantly towards the door. In walked the two judges. The organisers had somehow managed to get Rory MacAteer, the TV vet off 'Mac's Animals', as well as Mrs Mayhew-Carter who Dad said had been judging everything in Polgotherick since the Stone Age.

'She awarded me second prize in a fancy-dress competition when I was in primary school,' he said. 'Actually, I'm sure she was wearing that suit!'

It was a matching skirt and jacket with square shoulders, made of slippery material with a bright blue and green swirly pattern that made your eyes feel funny.

'Good afternoon, everybody!' said Mrs Mayhew-Carter, as soon as she was in position behind the judges' table. Rory MacAteer fell in beside her with his hands in the pockets of his famous brown combats, smiling broadly.

Mrs Mayhew-Carter gave a short speech which everyone listened to politely except for a Dachshund in the dogs' area that suddenly started barking and wouldn't stop. That was one dog who wouldn't be taking home any prizes!

They started with the cats. I don't know much about cats so I hadn't heard of any of the breeds except Burmese and Siamese.

Mrs Mayhew-Carter introduced each cat while its owner got it out of its travel box and brought it to the judges' table.

'Our first entry in this category is Gertie. She's a British Longhair, aged three.'

The judges looked at each cat standing up and sitting down. They asked the owner some questions and made some notes on their clipboards. Some of the cats didn't like it when the Dachshund started up again, but he was like a barking machine without a stop button.

The judges decided to do the dogs next. Maybe they were hoping the owner of the Dachshund might take him outside once he'd had his turn. The dog section was a bit different because as well as standing each dog on the table, asking questions and taking notes, the judges wanted to see the dogs walking to heel and obeying orders to sit and lie down.

After the dogs came the unusual pets. The boy with the tarantula dropped it before he got to the judges' table, which caused a stir, but it just sat there and waited for him to pick it up again. Maybe it was old, or lazy, or maybe tarantulas are the sloths of the spider world.

Mrs Bolitho's parrot refused to say 'Who's a pretty boy,' even when she kept prompting him. He was probably bored with the pet parade. I don't know where parrots come in the league table of cleverest animals, but I bet they're quite high up.

'Last but not least in this section, we have Pookie,' said Mrs Mayhew-Carter. 'He's two years old and he's a pot-bellied pig!'

Tammy unhitched his lead and led him towards the judges table. He couldn't stand on it because he'd break it, so the judges came round in front of it to look at him. Tammy said 'Sit!' and Pookie sat. She said, 'Lie down!' and he lay down. Then she walked him up and down in front of the judges before telling him to sit again.

Pookie looked very pleased with himself. The judges asked Tammy how long she had had him and some general questions about pot-bellied pigs. They were obviously impressed.

Mrs Mayhew-Carter reached back to get her clip-board off the table and Pookie's head shot up. His long snout got a whiff of something and he homed in like a sweet-seeking missile.

Gnash! Pookie sank his teeth into the bottom of Mrs Mayhew-Carter's jacket and pulled a huge chunk of the shiny material clean away. A half-eaten packet of Polo mints dropped out and rolled across the floor.

Mrs Mayhew-Carter screamed. Pookie lurched after the Polo mints, pulling Tammy right off her feet. The crowd edged two steps back, not knowing whether he was about to go on the rampage.

Rory MacAteer laughed and then got really embarrassed about it.

'It's not funny, young man,' snapped Mrs Mayhew-Carter. 'I've had this suit for twenty-five years!'

'I'm so sorry,' he mumbled, picking up the chunk of jacket Pookie had flung on the floor. 'Of course it's not funny. It was just a surprise.'

Pookie chewed up his Polo mints, wrapping and all, and then trotted back to his corner by the coat-pegs, dragging Tammy after him.

Mrs Mayhew-Carter patted her hair down and pursed her lips. She took a deep breath, and made some notes about Pookie on her clip-board. I don't suppose they were very positive.

The small pets were all a bit agitated by the commotion, shuffling and squeaking in their cages and travel boxes. Dennis didn't bat an eyelid at the screams and drama. He lives in the same house as Primrose, enough said.

The first small pet was a hamster called Gilligan. His owner was a very small girl with blonde fluffy hair and a lisp. When the judges asked her questions, she whispered her answers. 'He'th very nithe but he thleepth all day.'

When it was Heavenly Honeybun's turn the crowd oohed and aahed with admiration. Tammy put her carefully down on the judges' table. She was wearing cream-coloured leather gloves but they were much smaller than the gardening gloves so you hardly noticed them.

Heavenly Honeybun wouldn't sit still. She hopped to the front of the table and looked down. Rory MacAteer, seeing she was about to jump, reached out to stop her. She spun round and bit his finger.

'Ouch!' cried Rory MacAteer.

Thump! Heavenly Honeybun hit the floor running and raced for the door.

Becky pushed her sign-board across it just in time, so she had to divert. She whizzed round the edge of the hall. Tammy made a grab for her, hoiked her up into the air and carried her back to her travel-box, kicking like a kangaroo.

The audience were having a brilliant time but Mrs Mayhew-Carter and Rory MacAteer seemed to be going off the whole thing. She looked as if she was sucking a lemon as she announced that Dennis was next.

I carried him up to the front and put him gently on the judges' table.

I explained that he was a house rabbit, so he was used to being around people.

'He's very tame,' said Mrs Mayhew-Carter, stroking his ears.

Rory MacAteer hesitated, but then he reached out and stroked Dennis too. I could see that they liked him but they didn't say how beautiful he was or anything like that, so I decided to take a chance.

'He can do tricks,' I said. They didn't look convinced.

I had some rabbit treats in my pocket. They were in a tin so Pookie wouldn't be able to smell them. I gave one to Dennis and he gobbled it up. Then I took out another one and placed it gently on his nose. He sat completely still. He didn't try to eat it.

Way to show up poor old Pookie the pig!

Chapter 17
The First Cabbage Cake and the Friends you Want

You know when something so incredible happens that you actually can't believe it's true?

But then your family and friends come round your house for a celebration tea and, sitting down to eat the world's first cabbage cake, you suddenly realise it is?

Well that's what happened to me when Dennis won Best in Show at the Polgotherick Pet Parade.

I thought the game was up when the judges awarded Best Small Pet to Gilligan the hamster but I didn't mind. Dennis had done his best and I was proud of him.

But then Mrs Mayhew-Carter said, 'So now we come to the top prize, Best in Show, and we have decided to award it to Dennis the rabbit, who we feel could teach certain other animals rather a lot about nice manners!'

She shot Pookie a dirty look and Rory MacAteer glared at Heavenly Honeybun.

'Dennis is also the only rabbit we have ever seen who can do tricks, so we find him a most intelligent rabbit.'

It was nothing to do with intelligence, of course, it was just his rabbit nature, but I wasn't going to point that out. We went up to collect our prize. It was a silver cup with 'Polgotherick Pet Parade – Best in Show' engraved on it and a red rosette.

Mrs Mayhew-Carter handed me the cup and Rory MacAteer tried to rest the rosette on Dennis's front paws for the photographer. Dennis grabbed it in his teeth and started to eat it. I tried to get it off him, but he wasn't going to lose it like he did his good luck card. The photo in the Three Towns Gazette later in the week was of me trying to wrestle it off him.

Sasha, Tammy and Abina came up to congratulate me.

'Everyone's coming back to my house for tea,' I said. 'Would you like to come?'

They looked at each other in embarrassment.

'We've got tickets for the new Vampire Girl movie,' Sasha said. 'Sorry we forgot to tell you.'

I didn't mind – I was really glad! I didn't want to see Vampire Girl 2. I wanted to take Dennis home and make a fuss of him. I wanted to talk about the day with Toby and Jess, and find out how much money Becky had made for the RSPCA on her stall.

Mum said she had already made a special celebration cake because she had always been sure Dennis was going to win. It was a cabbage cake.

Gran remarked that she had never heard of cabbage cake and Mum said it was her own recipe, like carrot cake, but with cabbage.

'I've got three more cabbages to use up,' she said. 'You can take one home if you like.'

'Ooh, lovely!' goes Gran, but you could tell she didn't share Mum's enthusiasm for winter vegetables.

So there we all were, squashed in around the kitchen table, me, Becky, Jess and Toby, Mum and Dad, Primrose and Matt, Gran, Jane and

Mr Kaminski, eating cabbage cake and toasting Dennis's victory with fizzy lemonade.

And it suddenly hit me that this wasn't just a wonderful dream. Dennis really had won the top prize, we really were eating a cake made with cabbage, and I really had somehow managed to get all the friends I had offended back again.

'Have you missed your conference call with the agony aunts now, or are you doing it later?' Gran asked Dad. He shook his head.

'I don't think I'll be doing any more conference calls,' he said. 'The agony aunts are lovely, but they've got people skills and stuff, which I can't do at all, so we just don't really fit as friends.'

Dad said he reckoned friends were like shoes. You could have lots of pairs in the cupboard – your favourite trainers you wore most days and all the other ones you only wore sometimes like suit shoes, deck shoes or sandals.

But the point was, all your shoes had to fit. The ones you bought by mistake thinking they might stretch or your feet might get used to them – you always ended up taking them down to the charity shop.

Dad said he thought he had worked out how to get the friends who fit. Just be yourself, and then you would attract people who liked you the way you were and enjoyed the same sort of things.

We stared at him in astonishment, and then Gran said what we were all thinking.

'It looks like some of those people skills might have rubbed off!'

Will Primrose manage to squeeze into her dress? Will Dad cope when Ed tells him he's got to write a book? And will Peony get fit enough to go on a big adventure with Toby and Jess?
Find out what happens next in:

How to Get the Body you Want by Peony Pinker

And don't miss Peony's first two stories: